Cast of Characters

Uncle Aumbrey. A crafty, disagreeabl[e] nephews, whom he maliciously plays a[gainst] of his will.

Godfrey Aumbrey. The eldest nephew, who, until a recent revision, stood to in[herit]

Lewis Aumbrey. The other respectabl[e] architect.

Richmond Aumbrey. An impoverished poet, whose wife must work to help support their family. Nonetheless, he was once his uncle's favorite nephew.

Frederick Aumbrey. The black sheep of the nephews, a gambler, inveterate moocher, and aspiring blackmailer.

Professor Havers. A strange old man who dabbles in all forms of witchcraft.

Peter Piper. One of a trio of adventuresome undergraduates, flippant and fond of kittens.

David Harrison. Another undergraduate, also twenty, languid and sensitive.

Polly Waite. A student of law, thirty-two years old and the group's mastermind.

Dexter Catfield. A student who died a mysterious death.

Bluna. A black maid, formerly in the employ of Professor Havers.

Mr. S. Majestic. An educated black servant, also formerly employed by Havers, and engaged to Bluna.

Mrs. Beatrice Bradley. A well-known psychiatrist sleuth, interested in all things occult.

Inspector Ekkers. The investigating officer.

The Chief Constable. His superior, who frequently consults with Mrs. Bradley.

George. Mrs. Bradley's resourceful chauffeur.

Laura Menzies. Mrs. Bradley's lively niece and trusted secretary.

Celestine. Mrs. Bradley's French maid, quite wise in the ways of the world.

Old Mr. Catfield. Young Dexter Catfield's crotchety uncle.

Plus assorted servants, shopkeepers, policemen, and of course, Attila, the monkey.

Merlin's Furlong

A Mrs. Bradley mystery by

Gladys Mitchell

Rue Morgue Press
Lyons, Colorado

Merlin's Furlong

About Gladys Mitchell

Although some contemporary critics lumped Gladys Mitchell (1901-1983) with Agatha Christie and Dorothy L. Sayers as the "big three" of English women mystery writers, fewer than a third of her 67 books featuring Mrs. Bradley were published in the United States during her lifetime. But if she was not as well known on this side of the Atlantic as Sayers or Christie (or Ngaio Marsh, Margery Allingham, Patricia Wentworth, Josephine Tey, or Georgette Heyer for that matter), there was much in her prodigious output that has stood the test of tiime. In 1933 she became the 31st member of The Detection Club. In 1976, she was awarded the Crime Writers' Association's Silver Dagger.

During most of her writing career, Mitchell also taught English, history and games at various British public (here called private) schools. Her interest in athletics led to her membership in the British Olympic Association.

For more information on Mitchell and Mrs. Bradley please see Tom & Enid Schantz' introduction to The Rue Morgue Press edition of *Death at the Opera*.

To
Grace & Jules
with love

Merlin's Furlong

CHAPTER ONE

Merlin's Uncle

"The warp seemed necessity; and here, thought I, with my own hand I ply my own shuttle and weave my own destiny into these unalterable threads."

HERMAN MELVILLE—*Moby Dick*

In the first-floor turret room of an ancient and dilapidated house sat two men. One, who wore a handsome, old-fashioned smoking jacket and its matching, ridiculous cap, was dictating the terms of his will; the other, a neatly dressed, clean-shaven, dark-visaged man of forty, was jotting down its provisions with the effortless efficiency of long practice. On his face, which in repose might have been grim, was a bland, self-congratulatory smile.

"It's very good of you, uncle," he said at last, screwing the top on his pen and placing it in a narrow box which also held sealing-wax, a short taper and a propelling pencil. "I only hope the others will not think I have exercised influence."

"But you *have* exercised influence, my dear Godfrey," said the testator. "Great influence. You have exercised the influence of being the only one of the otherwise jealous and snarling pack of my relatives who has ever troubled to show me the slightest sign of affection, of care in my illnesses, of sympathy with my aims, my ambitions, and my undoubted loneliness."

"Oh, well, if that's the case, uncle, I'm very glad to have played my small part in making life tolerable for you. I know that since aunt died. . . ."

The benefactor raised a hand. It was a surprising hand for a gentleman of quality and education . . . large, coarse, and so hairy as to appear to be covered in fur. "Piltdown Man," another of his nephews had once called the owner of this hand. The nephew had not been forgiven and his name was not included among his uncle's beneficiaries, although, at that moment, he was staying in his uncle's house.

"Your aunt," said Piltdown Man, "was an exceptionally virtuous woman. But for her death, I might never have taken up my present extraordinary hobbies. In fact, I feel perfectly certain she would not have allowed me to do so."

"I thought you had only one hobby. Aren't you a collector of antiques, uncle?" The younger man looked demure and politely enquiring.

The collector of antiques chuckled.

"With a difference, my boy, with a difference! And that is not my only hobby, either."

"No?"

"No. And I must not forget that you are by profession wedded to the law. It would never do for me to tell you how I have come by most of my collection, nor what else I dabble in when I have the time to spare. But there's one thing I *will* do. Whilst you get those provisions put into a form which can be signed and witnessed, I'll go and get my latest treasure. It's the best thing yet, and the acquisition of it has given me peculiar satisfaction. So get on, my boy, whilst I go and prise it from its strongbox."

"You want me to draft your will *now?*"

"Certainly. It must be signed and witnessed this very night."

Mr. Aumbry, the sole survivor of a generation of Aumbrys who had been noted eccentrics, was, on the surface, a surprisingly normal old man, but, as his four nephews, who, from time to time, were invited to stay with him, had reason to know, beneath his outwardly placid and (except for his telltale hands), his almost pontifical appearance, he concealed a distorted personality and a crafty, criminal mind.

The respectable lawyer Godfrey, his eldest nephew, looked at him in silence for an instant . . . not longer, for he did not care to have the old man read his thoughts. Then he bent his gaze on his papers again and said quietly:

"So these are the provisions of your will?"

"Certainly, my boy. So, you see, you have nothing to fear. When I die you will be a wealthy man."

"But are you sure that, on thinking things over, you won't want to make some alterations? There's Lewis, for example. You haven't mentioned him so far." He shuffled his sheaf of notes.

"Neither shall I ever do so. Do you know what Lewis once called me?"

Godfrey did know, and had thought the title apt. He shook his head, however, preferring discretion to valor.

"Oh, well, I don't think I'll repeat it," said his uncle. He stretched out his ugly, hairy hands and flexed and unflexed their thick and primitive fingers. "And don't mention Richmond, either. Fate has dealt with *him*, I'm pleased to say."

"He's certainly very poor, and I think he's tubercular, uncle."

"All the better. I've no use at all for Richmond. Calls himself a poet! Expects to bring up those brats of his on doggerel! Lets his wife go out charring. . . ."

"Shorthand-typing, isn't it?"

"Tchah! Who cares what it is? Now you get my will set down properly, and when it's signed and witnessed I'll show you what I said I would. It's unique and it's priceless, and it was the apple of the fellow's eye who had it last! There's only one proviso. You must never tell anyone you've seen it, for I don't propose to show it to the others."

Godfrey was much too well trained in his profession to betray surprise. He nodded.

"Very well, uncle, if that's your wish. The provisions of the will are also, naturally, secret?"

His uncle made no reply. He felt in the pocket of the smoking jacket and produced a small chain purse. Jigging this up and down in his hand, he went out of the room. Godfrey spread out his notes, took a piece of paper from his briefcase, unscrewed his pen and set to work. He worked carefully and steadily for five minutes. The door behind him opened very slowly, an inch at a time, but he was absorbed and the intruder was very quiet. An upraised arm, a sudden, smashing blow, and the newcomer was scrambling the sheaf of notes together. In another instant he had gone, taking Godfrey's briefcase with him.

(2)

Mr. Aumbry and three of his nephews were at dinner. Upstairs a pale and heavy-eyed Godfrey was facing a plate of chicken and coping as best he might with a severe headache.

Around the dining table were Frederick, Lewis and Richmond Aumbry. The last two were brothers, although there was no family likeness between them and they were men of widely different character. Lewis, the elder brother, was a man of thirty-five, of moderate build and with a quiet manner and a cool eye. He had trained as an architect and had been reasonably successful in a profession to which, in his modest way, he was devoted. He accepted his uncle's fairly frequent invitations because he was genuinely sorry for the wicked and extraordinary old man. He was unmarried . . . the result of a girl's tragic death during his third year at the University . . . and his strongest feeling by far was for the young brother who sat facing him across the broad table.

Richmond Aumbry was a poet. He had never wanted nor intended to be anything else. He was excessively thin, with a fine head, dark-gray intro-spective eyes and the mouth of a voluptuary, although his passion was only for his Muse. He was married, fond of his wife and intensely selfish. He accepted his uncle's invitations because he literally needed good food and fine wines and could not afford to buy these for himself. His profession and his marriage both incensed his uncle, and the old man liked to have him at his table in order to gibe at him. A gift of protective cynicism gave Richmond the power to sustain himself in the face of this unkindness, and he rather enjoyed the cut and thrust of his conversation at table with the old man.

The third nephew was named Frederick. He took his looks from his mother, a Scandinavian, and was tall, blue-eyed and very fair. He had a high color, and was of an easy-going, amoral, slightly criminal temperament. He had always found his best friends among bookmakers and barmaids, even in his schooldays. He affected an attitude of ribald jollity, but could lose his temper on occasion, although never when the result would be to his own disadvantage.

Conversation at dinner on that particular evening concerned itself, naturally, with the unfortunate Godfrey and his injury.

"A nice thing!" exclaimed Piltdown Man. "Here I leave Godfrey with some most confidential documents, and one of you wretched thugs must needs come in and attack him and filch his papers! Who did it? Who did it, I say?"

The three men round the table looked at him and at one another. Then Frederick, who enjoyed play-acting, rose deliberately and flung his table napkin on to the floor.

"This is monstrous, uncle!" he said. "Before you bring these fantastic accusations, you might at least make some attempt to find out whether they are in any sense justified! Have you questioned the servants? Found anybody who saw one of us enter the turret room when Godfrey was there? Thought of the possibility that some outsider may be concerned? No! You don't like us, and so you wildly and criminally accuse us—or one of us—of having knocked poor old Godfrey on the head for the purpose of stealing his papers! What *were* these papers, anyway, that they appear to have so much importance in your eyes? You're not usually so tender-hearted about other people's property!"

"What do you mean by that, Frederick?" But the old man looked startled. He eyed his blond nephew anxiously. "What do you mean?" he repeated almost hysterically. Frederick nodded as though he was satisfied with the effect of his remarks. He kicked his chair back so viciously that it toppled over backwards, and strode out of the room. There was a moment's silence. At the end of it the front door slammed. The quiet Lewis got to his feet, picked up the chair, sat down again, and, leaning forward, said persuasively:

"Now, look here, uncle, Frederick has every reason to feel annoyed and insulted. So have Richmond and I. What makes you suspect any of us? What interest could Godfrey's papers have for us, unless he was drafting your will? . . . And I suppose he wasn't doing that!"

"Why shouldn't he have been doing that?"

"Oh . . . I see."

"You do, do you, Lewis?"

"I see, too," said young, thin Richmond. "But if he was drafting your will, uncle, you needn't, at least, suspect *me*. I know jolly well that I was cut out of it long ago. And if I could afford to buy my dinner I'd go and join Frederick in the village. As it is, I shall stay here and eat humble pie and your most delicious ragout." He smiled, winked at his brother and continued his meal.

"I'm glad you're not going, Richmond," said his uncle. "Godfrey is able, he thinks, to conclude his task this evening. The doctor does not anticipate serious consequences to follow that most cowardly and vicious attack on him; so, later—tomorrow morning, perhaps, if you will be so good—you and Lewis can witness my will. You rightly conclude that you are not to benefit."

"I'll witness your will for a tenner'," said the poet mildly.

"Nonsense!"

"A fiver, then. I'm not proud." He looked steadily at his uncle. "You sinful old man," he added suddenly.

(3)

"So you've changed your mind, uncle?" said Godfrey. "And Richmond is to benefit after all?"

"Just so, just so, my dear boy," Piltdown Man responded with enthusiasm. Godfrey was reminded of Dickens' Fagin.

"I suppose I've deserved it," he said. "Getting knocked on the head and my papers stolen, I mean." Except for extreme pallor which made his swarthy skin look dirty, he showed no particular marks of his experience. "I suppose you'll let him know? It is only fair."

"Certainly. But, my dear Godfrey, you must not take this too seriously. In a month's time I shall remake this will, employing a London solicitor and getting the will witnessed in Oxford, where I have many acquaintances."

"Including Professor Havers?"

"Including Professor Havers, about whom I could tell you a very droll story, except that it would not do."

"I'd like to hear it, uncle. Is the professor really as mad as one hears?"

"Mad? No, Havers isn't mad. At least, not in the sense you mean. In the American sense . . ." he chuckled with great malice . . . "as mad as ever a man can be. But, mad in the dictionary sense, no, he is not, and, in my opinion, never will be."

"Uncle, it's really no business of mine, but isn't it rather unkind to let Richmond think he will benefit at your demise if you really intend to revoke this will and make a new one?" asked Godfrey suddenly.

"You're too tender-hearted, my boy. My intention is that Richmond shall cause his wife to resign from her paid employment, that he shall realize upon his supposed inheritance and get himself into inescapable debt, that he shall presume to send his brats to a respectable school from which subsequently he will have to remove them for non-payment of fees, and that, finally, he shall die in a ditch with that wretched drab of his beside him!"

"I see, uncle." Godfrey looked thoughtfully at the hairy-fisted, scholarly-faced old man. "I shouldn't want you for *my* enemy."

His uncle chuckled.

"No fear of that, my boy. You're the only one of my kith and kin I care two straws about. And don't you worry. We'll get this document duly signed and witnessed, and then, next month . . . but, mind, this in sheerest confidence . . . a completely new will, putting you back in your proper sphere, the center and soul of my affections. But if I find you've been blabbing of this to the others. . . !"

"I shall keep all your secrets, my dear uncle," said Godfrey aloud. "And if I didn't, you wouldn't know it," he added silently.

The will was drafted, approved, signed in the presence of two servants who then witnessed the signature, and Richmond, called in to hear of the rise in his fortunes, was sent to the post with the completed document.

"For we'll have no more jiggery-pokery of people being knocked on the head to satisfy other people's curiosity," said his uncle. "And Wuloo is to go with you to the post office to make certain that you drop the envelope in the box, for I am not going to keep it in this house where people have such scant respect for other people's property."

"Very well," said Richmond. "And I think I'll look in at the village pub on my way back. If I can't afford to dine there, I think I might manage a small whisky in which to drink my own health. Oh, and yours, too, Uncle Aumbry, of course!"

"Whisky won't suit a man in your state of health," his uncle retorted. "Don't you want to live to enjoy your inheritance?" He caught the eye of his nephew Godfrey and smiled.

(4)

"But, I say, that's grand news! Congratulations, Rickie! I wonder what suddenly came over the old boy?" exclaimed Lewis when he had joined the new beneficiary in the public bar of the inn.

"Nothing came over him," said the poet quietly. "I've always taken one proverb to heart, old man."

"More than one, I hope?"

"One in particular. 'Beware of the Greeks when they come bearing gifts.' Ever heard it before?"

"Well, you'd better bash uncle's brains out before he has time to change his mind," said Lewis lightly. "And, talking of bashing, I wonder who *did* hit Godfrey over the head and pinch his papers this afternoon?"

"Your guess is as good as mine," said Richmond. "I only know who didn't, and that's either of us."

"I wonder?" thought Lewis. "The drinks are on me, old chap," he said aloud. "Down with the dram and to hell with Uncle Aumbry!"

"He'll end up there anyway," said Richmond. "You think Frederick hit Godfrey, then? He put on a good act of righteous indignation, but he's a born snooper, as we both know. But, I say, Lew, it would put me in the devil of a mess if Frederick did try the same game with uncle, and finished him off! I'd be hanged on the circumstantial evidence of having a fortune at stake, because it's most unlikely that uncle will allow this new will to stand. It's his way of getting at me, the miserable old humbug."

"I don't know so much. He always liked you much the best when we were boys. It wasn't until you decided to prefer poetry, and your own choice of a wife, to his (I suspect) rather shady business dealings and old Tom Mindenhofer's daughter, that you fell from grace, you know."

"Never to be picked up and reinstated, old man. But, you know, it *would* be serious for me if Frederick decided to go in for a night of the long knives, wouldn't it?"

"I shouldn't lose sleep over that," said Lewis quietly. "The only person Frederick will ever do anything for is himself. And you needn't count on *me* to do uncle in for you. I've far too much respect for the police and my own neck. Drink up, and let's have another."

"Not for me, Lew. The old devil was right about one thing. I'm in pretty poor shape, you know."

"I know," said his brother. "Why don't you pack up and go back to the sanitorium for a bit?"

"I hate it there. I can't work there."

"Don't they let you?"

"It isn't that. I just can't. And I'm on to a grand thing at present . . . easily my finest bit of work. I've talked things over with Phyllis and she's reconciled to my point of view. Oh, God, Lew! Why can't I do something for that poor kid! Why did she ever tie herself to a miserable, rotting, herring-gutted husband like me!"

"You know why," said his brother, "and it still holds good. And at least you two have had something that none of the rest of us have had. You wouldn't sooner have had my experiences, would you?" He ordered himself another drink, took a sip, and suddenly added, "Look here, old boy, go and have six months in Switzerland. You know I can find the money."

"You know I can't let you." The poet spoke with peevish haughtiness to disguise his real emotional response.

"You might go for Phyllis' sake if you won't go for your own," urged Lewis, turning his fine, intelligent eyes upon his brother. "I've never offered you two any money because I know what cussed proud devils you both are, but let me give her this."

"No!" said Richmond, almost violently. "I won't! I won't give in to this filthy, beastly disease! I'm going to finish my epic here, at home, in England!"

At this moment their cousin Frederick entered the bar and came up to them.

"Thought you'd have been here before this," said Lewis. "What will you have? We're drinking to Richmond's change of fortune."

"Change of . . . !" said Frederick coarsely. "You haven't really fallen for that stuff, Rickie, have you?"

"Hardly," replied Richmond. "By the way, what *did* make you hit old Godfrey over the head and rustle his papers? Did you think they'd give you a clue to uncle's treasure?"

"I?" Frederick looked surprised but not annoyed. "What on earth gives you the idea that I did that?"

"The science of deduction, with which is included the ability to do simple subtraction of the numbers up to ten," said Lewis. "We didn't do it, uncle presumably didn't do it, Godfrey didn't do it to himself, ergo. . . ."

"Well, I plead not guilty," said Frederick genially. "Pint of bitter, please. I'm dry. Wenching isn't quenching." He giggled victoriously.

"Wenching!" said Richmond in disgust as the brothers walked home, leaving Frederick in possession of the counter. "That's the village girls again, I suppose! Frederick isn't only a rotter in himself. He's got such execrable taste!"

"He has. I suppose he can't help it. Girls don't seem to take to him, and that doesn't give the lad much chance. He gets on well with barmaids, but they've far too much sense take him seriously."

"Do you think he's found uncle's *cache* yet? He's always hinting about ill-gotten treasure and such stuff."

"I wouldn't be surprised. And if he has, nothing will be safe from his pilferings. Uncle may be an old scoundrel, but I don't see why he should be robbed, especially by his own kith and kin. It isn't decent."

"Frederick's a headache, I know, but he does make money, which is more than I seem able to do. But there's something fishy about Godfrey's getting knocked on the head like that, and then uncle taking the notion of altering his will in my favor. I don't like it, and I'm skipping out of here as soon as I possibly can. If anything should happen to uncle before he reinstates Godfrey, I'm going to make certain of my alibi! Besides, I don't trust those slant-eyed Chink servants and that slippery Kanaka cook. Why can't uncle keep respectable English servants?"

"Nobody respectable would stay," said Lewis, laughing. "Nothing will happen to uncle. The devil takes care of his own. That's another proverb you might take to heart, you know."

CHAPTER TWO

Merlin's Doll

"To the hopeful execution do I leave you
Of your commission."

Shakespeare—Measure for Measure

In a large country house many miles from Mr. Aumbry's residence, three young men were variously engaged, none in a fatiguing, an ungentlemanly, or even a useful manner. Mr. Piper, flat on his back on the carpet, was playing with a Siamese kitten. Mr. Harrison was asleep in an easy chair. Mr. Waite was reading a newspaper.

"Something in *our* line, Peter," he remarked. Mr. Piper sat up, dislodging the kitten from his chest. He apologized crooningly. The kitten loved him with the paradoxical affection which her sadistic husband displayed for patient Griselda, and the paradox was italicized by the fact that the kitten was a female. As though to underline this accident of sex, by way of accepting his apology she bit his hand.

"Darling!" he observed reproachfully. The kitten leapt at him and dragged his tie out. He picked her up and placed her gently upon the bosom of the slumbering Mr. Harrison, whom normally she was inclined to mistrust. The kitten, true to her unpredictable *genus,* fell asleep at once, her paw engagingly linked with Mr. Harrison's breast-pocket.

"Something in *our* line, Polly?" said Mr. Piper, in a tone of distaste. "Oh, surely not. *I* don't want anything to do with anything whatever. What is a reading party for? To unbend the mind. Only that."

"This *will* unbend the mind," Mr. Waite pointed out. "Old Havers is at it again." He indicated with the stem of his briar an advertisement in the Personal column of the newspaper he had been reading. "And I know it must be Havers," he added, "because he's the only person except two who has ever believed that witchcraft would probably work."

"Except two?"

"Certainly. David here, and an elderly eldritch female, great-aunt to Bradley of Angelus. She's a bit of a witch herself, as a matter of fact . . . at least, so I hear on good authority. Gets people out of ghastly messes when nobody else can do a thing, or gets them hanged when nobody else thought them guilty."

"Oh, the sleuth! I know now. Rather a fascinating old party. I've met her.

Makes one feel an unlettered worm, but a rather nice, pink, well-intentioned worm. Bad for the morale and the ego, but stimulating to the digestive juices."

"You cannot separate the ego and the digestive juices," Mr. Waite contended.

"Don't sidetrack the conversation, Polly. So you think this must be Havers? Well, who else would be such a devil-worshipping, muddle-headed chump? Therefore, you are probably right."

"He may be a devil-worshipper . . . after all, the faculty must occupy itself *somehow,* one supposes . . . but I doubt very much whether he's muddle-headed or a chump. At any rate, he seems to have his knife into somebody, and it appears that he cannot say so publicly. Not uninteresting. Wake David."

"I will. Apart from the fact that we ought to include him in any discussion which is likely to be of general interest, I object to the sight of the only female I ever really loved dangling like a wilting lily from his breast-pocket. It's indelicate." He punched his sleeping friend in the stomach. The kitten leapt on his hand and bit it. Mr. Harrison, giving an histrionic belch, sat up with his hair on end.

"I've heard every word," he declared. "Ask Alice. I've heard every word you fellows were saying." With this he reassembled his loose form and closed his eyes again.

"No. Listen," said Mr. Waite impressively. "How would you like to visit Havers?"

"Why *should* I like to visit Havers? One can see him in term, and, anyway, I don't like him. He's decayed, dissolute, dreary and dreadful. He *eats* little children like me." Mr. Harrison's eyes remained closed.

"Yes, but, look, David dear." And Waite whacked the newspaper down on to Harrison's face. "You'll love this," he declared persuasively. "Really you will. Or shall Peter and I go alone?" he cunningly added.

Mr. Harrison gave in with utter grace. He handed the kitten to Piper and took the newspaper which Waite was now politely holding out.

"Where?" he enquired in meek tones; and when he had been shown the advertisement he read it aloud so that his friends should be certain that he really had seen it.

> "WANTED. Sorcerer, witch or warlock capable manipulating doll. Apply Nonsense, North Road, Wallchester, in person, with credentials. Undergraduates ineligible."

"Well, what about it?" asked Waite. Harrison put the paper down, yawned, and closed his eyes.

"No, no," said Piper earnestly. "We do really need your cooperation."

"You have it. You have it—but not for anything dark, dull, dirty or dangerous."

"It might be any or all of those, you know, Polly," said Piper. "And it's so nice here. Why do you always crave to *do* things? So much more gentlemanly simply to *be*. David is perfectly right. I exist," he continued dreamily, "thou existeth, he exists . . . although there seems no reason why he should. I now refer to our learned Professor Havers."

"He's a stinking old goat," said Waite in impartial tones, "and he's up to mischief, as usual. And I want to have a finger in the pie. This doll business is rather interesting."

"Why?"

"Oh, witchcraft fascinates and repels me, and I require to experience fascination and repulsion. Do wake David up and let's make plans."

Piper obliged by removing one of Harrison's shoes and striking him sharply on the kneecap with the heel of it. Harrison opened his eyes, rubbed his knee, put the shoe on again and sat up.

"That's better," said Waite. "Now, David, listen. I want to manipulate old Havers' doll. Peter doesn't want to. What do *you* think?"

"I don't want to think," replied Harrison after deep consideration. "Therefore, I say, let's go. And now, please, may I go to sleep again?"

"You may," Waite agreed. "Now, Peter, when shall we start?"

"Without delay."

"I agree. I could not stomach the dreadful disappointment of discovering that other and inferior witches and warlocks had got in before us and sneaked the job from under our noses. But, speaking as a practical man, what do you suppose it's all about?"

"I don't know. That queer business of young Catfield was never fully cleared up. I never really believed that it was suicide."

"I know. It stank. Did you ever go to Havers' rooms?"

"Yes, once, when he lived in College. He used to lord it over an earnest, smelly bevy of the long-haired. What they got up to I don't really know, but it wasn't anything savory. I heard lots of hints . . . everybody did, I expect . . . but until the Catfield business nothing much came out, and nothing was ever proved. One must give the devil his due. What about toddling over there tomorrow?"

(2)

Professor Havers lived in one of the most beautiful rooms to be found in the ancient cathedral and university city of Wallchester. The walls were paneled with medallions of carved oak in the style of the first quarter of the seventeenth century. The ceiling showed plaster decoration of the same period, displaying bold flowers and acanthus leaves in related but separated groups.

The carved overmantel was rated by connoisseurs as second only to that in the Principal's lodging in Jesus College, Oxford, and, although not quite so perfectly proportioned, was of much the same design and of approximately the same date.

The furniture in the room displayed a happy combination of styles. A Regency settee confronted a commodious, comfortable, modern one. A Sheraton table was not discountenanced by deep, well-cushioned armchairs. There was only one inescapably incongruous note. This was struck by a large, ridiculous doll which was hanging by the neck from a cheap and hideous hatstand of the kind that may be seen at the entrance to a hotel dining room. The doll was wearing plus-fours, a yellow waistcoat, a hacking jacket and carpet slippers. On its head was a check cap, and a small imperial had been glued to its chin. A collection of short hatpins had been stuck through various parts of its anatomy, and its imbecile face wore a look of vacuous astonishment, as though it protested at being subjected to this unkind, incomprehensible usage. It was, all told, a revolting as well as a ludicrous object.

It had been agreed that as Waite had had some previous acquaintance with the professor and was likely to be recognized, Piper and Harrison should conduct the negotiations whilst Waite remained in the street.

They were shown in by a Negro woman servant who lingered in the doorway, interested in the visitors. Her employer looked round and waved at her to go away. With a shrill squeal, half of fear, half of laughter, she fled.

"A happy chit," said Professor Havers indulgently. His printed silk dressing-gown, patterned mosaically in gold and bright blue, accorded with his Eastern Roman countenance. "And now, gentlemen, what can I do for you?"

Piper said courteously, "We've come to see a man about a doll."

The professor's large-eyed, spiritually beautiful face began to brighten, but not to its aesthetic advantage, for two yellow wolf-teeth appeared with Satanic effect.

"Sit down," he said. "My dear sirs, *do* sit down." He indicated the object on the hatstand. "There is the person in question. Its name is Aumbry, Nabob Aumbry, Collector Aumbry, Thief Aumbry. He stole my diptych, my Isaurian diptych, and he denies that he's got it, and I've no proof that it really is in his possession. *But he's got it, and he shall die.*"

He pronounced the last sentence with the greatest possible earnestness and intensity. A cold breeze blew suddenly on to the back of Harrison's neck. He glanced round, but the door behind him was closed. Piper was gazing fixedly at the doll as though to imprint its appearance on his memory.

"I think, sir," he said, "that you should describe the diptych in detail. It might be as well that we should know what we are looking for."

"But I didn't . . . I don't expect to see the diptych again. It was the doll," said Havers, his querulous, complaining voice belying his saintlike appearance as much as his smile had done. "I thought you would make the doll work. Are you not witches and warlocks?"

"Witches only," Piper courteously replied. "In disguise, of course," he added, indicating Harrison's large trousers.

"We left the blasted heath at home," said Harrison, with ill-timed levity. His friend rewarded him with a surreptitious hack on the shin.

"To be plain with you, sir," he said, gravely, "we propose to use the doll to recover the diptych."

"But that won't work," protested the professor. "The doll is for the untying of Aumbry's life-knot, not for recovering the diptych."

"There is such a thing as frightening a man into giving up stolen property," said Piper. "That is how we modern witches work. The method you are employing"—he strolled over to the doll—"is out of date. Now tell me all about the diptych."

"It is famous," said Havers peevishly. "It is the Isaurian diptych, so called because it was made in defiance of the edict of Leo the Isaurian that the Second Commandment should be observed to the very letter, and neither image nor statue, picture nor representation be made of anything in heaven or earth. It was the bishops' fault," he concluded violently. "Imagine iconoclastic bishops in the city of Constantine the Great! Puritans at the apex of the Eastern Roman Empire! Infidels anticipating the Camel Driver of Mecca! Gah!"

"And the description of the Isaurian diptych?" persisted Piper, with a patient, gentle smile. The professor sighed heavily.

"Ah, yes, the diptych," he said. "No doubt you are interested to know what it looks like. Well, it is of great intrinsic value, apart from its historic worth. It is of gold and enamel, and dates, as you will realize from what I have already said, from about 730 A.D., Leo's famous edict having been proclaimed some four years earlier. Another name for it is the Ravenna diptych, for it reproduces four of the most famous mosaic pictures to be found in the churches there, and the artist was almost certainly a native of that place although he may have been domiciled for a time in Constantinople.

"The diptych, as I told you, is of gold. The decorations enameled on the inside leaves represent the mosaic pictures of, on the top half of the left-hand leaf, the Emperor Justinian clad in purple, crowned with a coronet of red, blue, green and pearl, making his offering of a gold cup to the Church of San Vitale. On the lower half of the same leaf is an exact copy in miniature of the charming decoration patterned with stylized lilies, small roses, and birds of variegated plumage, which is to be seen in the vaulting of the forecourt of the archi-episcopal chapel and the oratory of Saint Andrew in Ravenna. You will fully realize the beauty of this patterning against the flat bright gold of the background."

There was no doubt now of the intense interest of his hearers. Even the flippant Piper was impressed. The sensitive Harrison had his mouth open, and was leaning slightly forward, his forehead creased in a frown of concentration.

"The top half of the right-hand leaf," continued the professor with animation, "is a perfect representation of the Empress Theodora and her court. She also is offering a cup to San Vitale, and the coloring of this picture is truly exquisite, from the detail of the Three Kings of the Orient on a band of embroidery on the hem of the purple robe worn by the Empress, to the tiny blue flowers on the golden dress which is worn by one of her ladies. On the lower half of this leaf is some decorative detail from the barrel vault of the mausoleum of Galla Placidia. This decoration is in brilliant white stars and red and white roses in circles of blue and gold, all this against a background of indigo. Oh, it is ravishing! Ravishing!" His voice suddenly changed. "And that fool, that devil, has stolen it, and for that desecration he shall die!"

"Good show," said Piper in businesslike tones, "and now, sir, for Mr. Aumbry's address."

The professor went over to a small bureau, unlocked it, produced an address book, thumbed it over and dictated: "Merlin's Furlong, Moundshire. That's it. That's where Aumbry lives." He went to the doll and threw the address book at it. Having done this, he glowered at the doll, dragged out the hatpins and shook his fist in the doll's face. "Do your worst," he concluded.

"Our best, I think you mean," said Piper. "Very good, sir. I suppose we shall find this Mr. Aumbry at home?"

"Still here," said the professor morosely. "How, otherwise, do you think I could have obtained his hair with which to decorate my doll? Fortunately we patronize the same barber."

"Then he is still in this very city?" Piper enquired.

"So far as I know. Go, gentlemen, and the good luck of Priapus go with you."

They left, shown out by the Negro maidservant, who had obviously been listening at the door. Another shining dark face, split by an ivory grin, peered at the departing visitors from behind a curtain of beads which hung across the hall.

"What now?" asked Piper, as they walked the short distance to a bus stop, where, by previous arrangement, they met Waite.

"To lunch, and then home," said Waite, with immense relish, when he had heard their story.

"Then what?" demanded Harrison, who again felt the call of slumber.

"Then you are going to become a cat burglar, dear," replied Waite. "You are going to shin up water-pipes and crawl in through window-cracks nine floors up from the ground. You are going to insinuate yourself and those indecently hirsute trousers into the plug-holes of baths and wash-basins, and from those plug-holes you are going down, down, down . . . down! Won't that be nice? Aren't you glad you sold your little farm and went to sea?"

"Look here, you're not really going any further with this dreary, dirty little business, are you?" asked Harrison apprehensively. His friends looked surprised.

"My bite is worse than my bark," Waite informed him, "and my bark is simply dreadful. Have you never been bitten by a cat-burglar, dear?"

"If you ask *me*," said Harrison soberly, "the biter is going to be bit, but I suppose you've both made up your minds."

"Here comes a bus," said Waite. They mounted and rode to the center of the city. As soon as they got off, Piper, who was still holding the doll, walked into the middle of the street and harangued the effigy of the unknown Mr. Aumbry in Greek, answering himself from time to time in a high, ridiculous voice as though he were practicing ventriloquism. At intervals he wiped the doll's nose, disregarding entirely the rapidly-collecting crowd on both pavements and the looming figure of the law.

"Move along there, sir, *please,*" said the law. "You are causing an obstruction."

Piper kissed the doll passionately, thrust it with a low sob into the policeman's arms, and, leaping like a deer, rejoined his companions on the pavement, and they moved with dignity towards the hotel where they proposed to have lunch. The policeman, who was just going off duty, took the doll to the police-station. For one thing, he was doubtful whether it had really been Piper's own property, and, for another, he was not at all sure that it was the sort of thing to appeal to his little girl.

"I'm not sure you ought to have parted with the doll," said Waite to Piper. "It was a kind of talisman, you know. I don't see how we are to obtain the desired result without it."

"Be your age," said Piper.

"I'm thirty-two," said Waite. Harrison, who knew this to be the truth, felt thoroughly uneasy. He and Piper were twenty, an age at which ragging, he felt, was a serious, necessary business. That Waite, who was known to have knocked about all over the world before he decided to read law at the university, should also take ragging seriously seemed rather in the nature of a fully-grown dog taking pleasure in the puppy antic of chewing a shoe.

"Cheer up, David," said Piper, as the three young men sipped sherry, "even if you *would* rather have beer. This idea of Polly's is quite good, on the whole."

"I can have beer with the lunch," said Harrison, "and I'm not at all sure that it *is* a good idea. Suppose old Havers is leading us up the garden, and there isn't a diptych at all?"

"Then we shall look fools," said Waite cheerfully. "Anyway, it will be something to *do,* and that's always worth while."

"Not to me. I merely want to eat and sleep," said Harrison. "And my parents won't like me to become a cat burglar."

"Yes, they will. They'll be ever so proud of you," said Waite. "Who's paying for the next round? Is it my turn? Yes, I was afraid it was."

CHAPTER THREE

Merlin's Error

"There must surely be great cause for secrecy when so many inconveniences were confronted to preserve it."

Robert Louis Stevenson—*The Pavilion on the Links*

Piper's enthusiasm had waned with the passage of time. "You know, it's a social crime to rag anybody as gullible as old Havers, devil-worshipper or whatever you will," he said. "You'll never be able to get your hands on that diptych, I didn't at all like that doll, and, anyway, you won't get David to come in." He contemplated his sleeping friend. They were back where they had started. It was late at night and, although they were still up, Harrison's long form was supine and his breathing was deep and regular.

"Rag Havers?" asked Waite. He put down the motoring atlas he had been studying. "My dear chap, what gave you the idea that I'm ragging? I am, of course, in a sense, but about the project itself I am deeply and unfashionably serious. I fully intend to break into Merlin's Furlong . . . it will be some decayed, mildewed dump, if I know anything of Havers' acquaintances . . . and creep about like the family ghost until I spot the diptych, which I have no doubt is there. I shall simply impound it and restore it to its owner."

"We shall be jugged. Besides, it's all such rot. Why should we sweat?"

"Because I want to. There's no need for you to come, although I could do with somebody at the wheel of the car for when I make my dash away with the treasure."

"The car? Oh, we're not going to *drive!*"

"Can't cat-burgle without a car," said Waite decisively. "And I note, to my relief, the use of the first person plural, so you'd better check the route with me. It's all right as far as Moundbury, but then it looks all 'other roads' as the Ordnance Survey so euphemistically and optimistically calls them. And as we're going to drive we'd better try to get the hang of them. I think we ought to get there by dawn and have a good look at the place before Aumbry and his people are up."

"Aumbry's away from home, that's one thing."

"He may not still be away. I'm going to assume that he isn't. Actually, I hope to goodness he isn't."

"Why?"

"I'm going to take a leaf out of Sherlock Holmes' book, laddie."

"If you mean that gag about the dog that did nothing in the night, I should say that, if Aumbry's got a dog, it won't apply."

"I do not refer to the dog that did nothing in the night, but to the psychology of the most precious possession."

"Oh, Irene Adler! But if you begin raising a fire in Aumbry's place for the satisfaction of seeing him make one leap for the diptych, you'll probably get ten years. Besides, the diptych may not be his most precious possession."

"I do not propose to raise a fire. I should never dream of such a thing. I shall simply raise the cry, and, if David comes, I shall get him to ring the stable bell . . . a dump called Merlin's Furlong is sure to have one."

"Don't you believe it," said Harrison, opening his eyes. "Either melted down for cannon balls in the Civil War or collected as scrap metal for this last one."

"Oh, well, never mind the bell. We can toot on the horn of the car," said Waite, as Harrison relaxed once more. "Now, look here, Peter, the basic idea simply is that we get down to the job at night and are back here again before there's a hue and cry. Not that there will be. If this man Aumbry has pinched the thing from Havers, he won't care to create a stink if it's taken back. You must see that. The whole point is that I've always wanted to do a cat-burglary, and now that the chance has presented itself it would be a sin to throw it away. Besides, I want to know more about Havers. He's an interesting social study."

"All right," said Piper. "I'd better wake David."

The planned route took them through Wallchester, where it seemed a good idea to Waite to leave Professor Havers a short note to inform him that they were setting out upon their quest. The note, written by Harrison, was put through the letter-box at an early hour of the morning and the car ran on into Faringdon. Here Waite recollected that he had an aunt, so, at a time unexpected by any respectable householder, this aunt received visitors.

She proved to be a sardonic, muscular woman of forty-five to fifty who herself answered the front-door bell. She appeared in a striking orange and cobalt dressing-gown and she flourished a murderous-looking *kukri*. Fortunately for him and his companions, she recognized her nephew before her weapon came into action.

"Off with his head," she said, lowering the *kukri* as though this order had been complied with. "I've no food and no beds. Come in. Oh, wait a minute." She took a minute sliver of skin from her wrist with the razor-edge of her weapon and drew blood. "That's a superstition or a tradition. I forget which," she said. "Anyway, it has to be done. Ritual must always be observed."

They supped upon cold chicken and champagne, and breakfasted on rashers, eggs, baked beans and sausages, and by eight o'clock in the morning there was a general feeling that bed was not only desirable but essential. The aunt, who had remained with them throughout the revels, discovered two spare beds and a settee. This last had an end that let down. The cat burglars retired to rest and resumed their journey at midday. After lunch they went on in the late afternoon to Moundbury, the capital of Moundshire, and, after that, lost the way. Waite was driving.

"You're doing it on purpose," said Harrison lugubriously to Waite. "Why not admit to cold feet and let's go home? Second thoughts are always the best."

"You can't have the best of only two," argued Piper. "Let's go back to Moundbury and have dinner."

When this was eaten they received some confused directions from the porter, who affected to know the place they mentioned (but referred to it throughout as Merlin's Castle), and set out once more upon their quest.

"You know," said Piper, at the end of fifteen miles of hilly side-roads, "either this map is wrong or the landscape's got itself bewitched. I'll swear we passed that circle of standing stones five miles back."

"I keep expecting to see somebody in woad and a helmet with horns on it pop out and lob a chunk of limestone or an iron spear through our windscreen," said Harrison.

"I think that hotel porter was a loony," said Waite. "We've done exactly as he told us, and if he was right we could have found the place twice by now. Do you think it's any good going on?"

"I think we ought to go back and start again from where you turned off the Sherborne road," said Piper. "I thought that was wrong, but I trusted to your native intelligence. It is, perhaps, a mistake to think you have any. It makes me wonder, too, whether we heard the address Havers gave us quite correctly."

"The porter knew Merlin's Furlong, except that he kept calling it a castle, which I don't really think it can be," said Harrison, "but we've certainly come the wrong way. I'm still in favor of packing up the whole thing. It's quite clear that we're not *intended* to find the diptych, and I'm very superstitious. I never dream of tilting against my luck. It's always disastrous."

"I'll turn the car as soon as I can," said Waite. "There seems nothing for it but to do as Peter suggests, and get back on to the main road and ask again. Why can't people who are going to be cat-burgled live in some sensible, get-at-able place such as Bournemouth or Harrogate? But give up the job I will not!"

By nightfall the three undergraduates, still driven by Waite, who refused to give up the wheel, were bumping along a rough track-way bordered by wire fencing. They were following the direction of a signpost which bore the tantalizing legend, MERLIN'S FORT ONLY. UNSUITABLE FOR MO-TORS.

"Well, I'm dashed!" said Harrison. "It *must* be the place we're looking for, but it looks as though this old man Aumbry doesn't care for visitors."

"I don't know so much. Merlin's Fort isn't quite the same as Merlin's Furlong," argued Piper. "What do *you* think, Polly?"

Waite did not answer, and Harrison continued his criticism.

"As soon as people begin to say that a road is unsuitable for motors I can't help feeling what they mean is that they don't really *want* motors, and here we are, *in* a motor. Isn't it asking for trouble? I mean, I do hate to push myself in where I'm not welcomed," he complained. "And it's got so confoundedly dark. We shan't be able to see anything, even if we *do* somehow find the beastly place."

At last the wire fence ended, and the headlamps picked out a vast, uncharted, boundless, uninhabited plain. It was as though the car had been transported to the middle of an unmapped continent. The road, such as it was, petered out, and the car, still bumping, ran on to virgin turf, and Waite decided to stop.

"What are you stopping for?" demanded Piper.

"Because we're going to sleep in the car," Waite replied. "We're up against Mount Everest, I think."

"Something *does* seem to be looming," said Piper, peering through the windscreen.

Harrison, who had the back of the car to himself, opened the near-side door and got out. The moon, which, hitherto, had been screened, except intermittently, by cloud, swam into a patch of clear sky. Beneath her light, an asymmetrical and awe-inspiring mass rose, menacing and eerie, before him. Contrasting shadows of blue-black, gray, and greenish-purple indicated depressions and indentations in the mass, and at one point, directly in front of the car, there rose a causeway, verdant in the moonlight, which seemed to lead to some ghostly sanctuary.

Harrison returned to the car, got in, and shut the door with a boom which seemed to rebound from the grisly hill.

"It's Merlin's Fort, all right, I should think," he said. "It looks like some dashed great earthwork, and it's probably haunted."

"Better explore it, then," suggested Piper. "I'm sick of sitting in this car."

"You'd break your neck," said Harrison. He seized the only rug, disposed himself along the back seat, and, as usual, wooed and won the welcome bride, sweet slumber.

"Well, I'm dashed!" said Piper. "What does David think we can do on these two bucket seats? Shall we wake him up and throw him into the night?"

"Not so, but far otherwise," responded Waite. "Look, Peter, back there a bit I think there's a whole lot of heather. Pinch the rug back from David and we'll toss for it, the other to take the raincoats. Then you and I will doss in the heather. I've done it before and it's certainly much more comfortable than the two front seats of the car."

"Right," agreed Piper. He took away Harrison's rug without disturbing that gifted sleeper, and he and Waite tossed up by the light of Waite's torch. Waite won, but elected to take the two raincoats.

"I'd like one to roll up for a pillow," he explained.

Harrison was the first up when day dawned. He crept out of the car, discovered, without surprise, the sleeping-place chosen by his companions, and climbed the hill to explore the Iron Age fort. Upon descending he met a forlorn-looking man who exchanged greetings with him. Harrison followed these up by enquiring the way to Merlin's Furlong. The man denied any knowledge of the place.

"Merlin's *Castle,* like, and this be no sort of a way, if you comes in a car, to get to she," he said definitely. He passed on, a silhouette against the sunrise. Harrison gazed after him and then returned to his friends, whom he found still asleep in the heather. He roused them. Waite looked hollow-eyed, and Piper confessed he felt stiff. There was nothing to eat, and around them stretched the primitive landscape, agonizingly desolate, desolately beautiful, like the Spanish princess who had lost her lover. Before them stood the stark, long-abandoned stronghold of Merlin's Fort; behind them was the fickle and bumpy road over which they had previously journeyed. Waite sighed, and turned the car round.

"Nothing now but a miracle . . ." he said. "Anyway, I'm hungry. If we can find anywhere for breakfast we'll stop and have it." The car bumped back along the trackway, and soon overtook the man to whom Harrison had spoken. Waite pulled up.

"Breakfast?" said the man. "Well, you baint very far from Moundbury." He gave them precise directions.

"Well, I'm hanged!" exclaimed Harrison. "Polly, you chump, you've been driving us round in circles!"

"Sorry," said Waite without betraying contrition. "Never mind. You can take the wheel now, if you like."

The car gained the highroad and headed again for Moundbury. A late breakfast and another interview with the hotel porter followed. Nothing was gained. The porter declared that the gentlemen had enquired the way to Merlin's Castle. The gentlemen were equally insistent that they had asked for Merlin's Furlong. Deadlock was reached. Harrison, who, all along, had had very little stomach for the business, again and again urged that they should return home, but Waite was insistent that Merlin's Furlong existed and must be found. They decided to leave the matter until after lunch, feeling the need for arm-chair slumber in the lounge. By this time, too, both Piper and Harrison were in favor of assuming that Aumbry's house was Castle, not Furlong, and that they should accept the porter's directions as being correct and use the rest of the daylight for following them.

The car then set off once more, Piper, in the back seat, declaring loudly and beerily that love would find a way. Waite, determined and frowning, sat beside Harrison, who was driving. They turned northward because Harrison had a secret theory that if they could once strike the main road from Marl-borough all his troubles would be at an end and he could drive his compan-ions half-way home before Waite discovered what was happening.

His luck was out. Before the car had covered seven miles there was a signpost which showed, by implication, that they were going in the right direction. It read: MERLIN'S HAZARD 5. BLOODPUDDLE 7. PENNY-ROYAL 9. MERLIN'S ELL 12.

The miles were long ones, and the road was hilly. The car drove through the signpost-named villages, which seemed asleep, and across the checkered landscape with its prehistoric entrenchments and sacred sites, its round bar-rows and its ancient terraced fields, until at last a high stone wall cut off the view to the left. The road marched with this for more than a mile. It seemed to be the boundary wall of a very considerable park, and was broken by an occasional wooden door.

The wall cast a deep shadow over the road, and Waite, who had been keeping a keen eye on their progress, seemed depressed as he commented upon the height and the apparent length of it. He announced that he was battling with his first doubts as to the advisability of their mission. Harrison drove on at a reduced speed. He was hoping that the wall would not disclose an open gate. The wall let him down.

"Here we are," said Piper, as the wall gave way to an unguarded opening. "This is it, I feel certain." Harrison, the tool of Fate, took the turning and the car ran slowly past a deserted lodge and up a long, unweeded gravel drive. "At least" . . . Piper's confident tones gave way to more hesitant utterance . . . "I suppose it is, but it looks such a whacking great place."

His stupor, due to the beer, had worn off, and he was sitting forward, peer-ing between the shoulders of the two in front.

"It must be," agreed Waite. "There's one thing" . . . he stared critically at the house through the wind-screen . . . "it ought to be easy enough to get in."

The house was, in size and grandeur, far beyond any of their expectations . . . a huge pile of Jacobean architecture with a dry moat surrounding it and a handsome, ornate stone bridge (which led to a double doorway the width of a minor road) spanning what had once been water.

"Shocking big place," insisted Piper; and there was indeed something shocking in all that decayed and mullioned grandeur.

Over the magnificent doorway was a pillared porch, part of which represented the full achievement of a peer of the realm, escutcheon, coronet, helmet, crest, mantling and motto. This porch formed a balcony to a long window which had four lights of equal width divided from one another by a narrow framework of stone. One of the lights had lost most of its glass.

"Too easy to be interesting," said Harrison, hoping that the very simplicity of the task in view would deter his misguided friends. As he spoke, a man carrying a small portmanteau came into view at the side of the house and walked towards them. He was respectably dressed in a black jacket and striped trousers, and wore an unimpeachable bowler.

"Jeeves in person," said Piper, and advanced a step or two to meet him. "I do hope we are not intruding," he said, courteously.

"Not at all, sir," the man civilly and quietly replied. "No doubt you know we are up for sale. If you have an order to view. . . ."

"Er, I'm afraid not, no. A very fine old place, though. You must be proud to live in it."

"Indeed, yes, sir. But it wants a lot of keeping up, these days, and sell we must, so if you should care to ask for an order to view I could show you round before I leave. Without it, I could scarcely venture."

"Of course not," said Waite. "Look here, can we give you a lift with that bag as far as the station?"

"Very kind indeed of you, sir." The man picked up his portmanteau, which he had set down during the conversation, and it was soon in the boot. He himself was given the spare seat, and the party of four drove back on to the road and were guided by the manservant towards a branch-line station about two miles out of the tiny hamlet which the young men had already passed through, and which was called Merlin's Ell.

"I believe your employer is a collector of antiques," remarked Piper, who was sharing the back seat with the man.

"He used to be, sir . . . at least, the *old* gentleman was. But there's nothing like that now. Pictures, ornaments, trophies . . . they've all had to go the same way. I'm the only manservant left, and we used to have a staff of thirty in my grandfather's time. Now there's only me, the cook, and a couple of maids, but the master's away a good deal of the time, so we manage."

"I suppose most of the house is shut up, then?"

"Nearly all of it, sir. Just except for two or three rooms in case there's company, and our bedrooms and the kitchen, of course, and the master's own room. It comes easier that way, but it's a sad thing, sir, to see a great house in decay."

They dropped him at the station, received renewed and courteous thanks, and drove off, still traveling away from the house. This was at Piper's suggestion.

"Don't want to give him the impression that we're going back there," he observed. "We're sure to find a turning somewhere that will take us back along another road. Mistake to have given him a lift, in a way, because he'll remember us. Still, we had to get rid of him, I suppose. Bit of a nuisance meeting him, all the same." He relapsed into a thoughtful silence which was shortly broken by Waite.

"One thing, with him out of the way, there will be nobody to cope with except Aumbry and the women-servants," he observed. "It's a bit of a sitter, isn't it?" He sounded so disconsolate that Harrison said hastily:

"Too much of a sitter altogether, Polly. What about turning it up?"

"Not on your life," said Waite. "I said I'd get the diptych back, and I'm going to do it. After all, if the job had turned out to be really sticky (which it may still do if Aumbry packs a gun, and these country cousins usually do) we shouldn't have given it up, so I don't see. . . ."

"Oh, all right," said Harrison in despair. "We shall all get jugged, but what of it? I shall look forward to seeing you with your little pick-axe and wearing your nice new Government suit with the pretty markings."

"Did he have cold feet, then?" asked Piper. He changed his tone. "As a matter of fact, so have I. But we can't back out, David. I agree with Polly there. Tell you what, though, Polly," he added, "the difficulty is not to get into the place . . . you could do that in your sleep . . . but to find the diptych. It might be anywhere, and is probably in Aumbry's bedroom. Had you thought about that?"

"Yes," said Waite. "But I've got an old Army revolver in with the tool kit. I shall take it with me and hold the thieving old jackdaw up if I can't get the diptych any other way."

"Oh, Lord! Don't be such a fool!" said the unhappy Harrison. "If that's your idea you'd better let *me* do the job. Yes, now, Polly, look here, you stay below to catch the thing when I drop it. I'm a good bit taller than you, and can skid quicker from that porch if pursued. And at least I wouldn't be fooling about with revolvers."

"We could both go," said Waite, as though struck by a brilliant idea. "The place is too big. Yes, we'll split up the rooms between us. Be a whole heap quicker that way. I don't suppose for a minute that Aumbry keeps the diptych in his bedroom. Why should he? He'd never think of anybody coming like a thief in the night to get it back. Look, let's do that if you think you can be reasonably catlike. I've brought a couple of string bags which will slip over our wrists and not get in the way when we're climbing down again. Then we need not have anybody below to catch the thing, and that will also avoid any chance of damaging it. Peter will have to be ready to start the car at a second's notice, and here, I hope, is a play fitted. What comments, if any?"

"Well, as you seem to be set on it, I suppose there's no point in arguing. There's only one thing. I hope the women won't set up a screaming, for that I could not abide."

"Oh, Lord! I'd forgotten women might do that. We shall just have to throttle them, that's all, although murder is hardly the recognized behavior of cat burglars, and might be a union matter."

"Then you'll do the strangling," said Harrison. "Fancy trying to choke a lymphatic cook-general of fifty! If they scream, I shall run like a rabbit."

"Don't anticipate events. Where's this turning we rather optimistically counted on? One thing, as that fellow in the bowler had his bag, he won't be coming back. Better turn the car at this next gateway, David. The chap must have disappeared by now."

Harrison turned the car, and, driving with exemplary care (for he did not propose to get back to the house an instant before he need), at last he brought the party once more to the open gateway.

"I'm hungry," he said, as he pulled up. "What about driving on?"

"Not on your life," said Waite. "We brought plenty of grub from Moundbury to last the night. Drive in. If anybody comes and shoos us off, we'll park the car on the other side of that hill and sneak back as soon as they've gone."

Harrison, shrugging hopelessly, and finding uninspiring and fearful visions of Dartmoor in his mind, drove very slowly through the gates. The three young men got out and concealed themselves in the bushes. Piper picked a few leaves and put them on the bonnet of the car, but decided that they did not disguise her.

"Don't play the fool, Peter," said Waite. "Keep watch and ward. I don't like the look of this business. If there are women servants about, surely *one* of them heard the sound of the car!"

"I expect they're all murdered in their beds, and the bag that man was carrying contains their heads," said Piper. "If so, we're accessories after the fact for aiding and abetting his escape by carrying, conveying and devil-portering him to a railway station, goods-siding or permanent way, to the detriment, destruction and disintegration of the law of the land and the peace of Her Majesty's subjects."

"It's not at all nice," said Harrison, "and I *still* want my dinner."

"Stand by for a bit," said Waite. "I'm going to do a spot of sleuthing. There *must* be somebody about, if it's only a caretaker."

CHAPTER FOUR

Merlin's Folly

"There have I made my promise to call on him
Upon the heavy middle of the night.

SHAKESPEARE—*Measure for Measure*

Waite returned without any information except to report that there seemed no sign of life anywhere. The three young men waited and watched, but no tradesmen or visitors called, no servant, either man or woman, appeared, and nobody worked in the garden. Harrison, at seven o'clock, again announced that he wanted his dinner, and produced potato crisps, cheese rolls, half a chicken, two cold fishcakes, a lobster sandwich, a cucumber and some bottled beer. The others unrolled equally interesting meals and all three drank Harrison's beer.

"Well, now," said Waite, when the diverse repasts were over and they had sneaked out on to the road and lighted their pipes, "as I say, I don't much like the look of things, but it's easy enough to get in, and it will be easy enough to get out. No one seems to be about, which is extremely odd, but the servants may be on board wages and that man we met may simply be going on his holiday. Still, it's queer that there isn't so much as a caretaker in the place."

"So it's just a case of laying hands on the diptych," said Piper, in the easy tone of one who knew that this was not to be his task. Waite nodded, pulled at his briar for a moment or two, and then said, stabbing the air with its stem:

"It's a much bigger house than I had supposed. I suggest we crack it at dusk. There's a lot of heavy cloud coming up. I think we're in for a storm."

"Let's hope there's plenty of thunder, then," said Harrison. "Anything that helps to drown our noises and create a diversion will be welcome. *I* don't believe the house is empty. It doesn't *look* empty, somehow."

"Look here," said Piper, whose indulgent fondness for kittens was sometimes, although not often, extended to the human race, "I'll climb with Polly, if you like, David, and you can handle the car."

"No. I'd go to sleep at the wheel, and then we might all be nabbed," responded Harrison. He looked up at the lowering sky. " 'A foul bombard that would shed his liquor.' Polly's right. It's going to be the brute of an evening."

The rain began at eight, but there was no thunder. There was still not a sight or a sound of anybody up at the house, and no lights were showing. There was a break in the heavy sky to the north-east, and through it glared malevolently a lurid setting sun. It burned in the diamond casements of the house like a conflagration, and Harrison's long, lean body shivered with apprehension as he looked at it.

"The Ides of March," remarked Piper, following his gaze. "Cheer up, David, dear. It will all be over by to-morrow!"

" 'Would it were bedtime and all were well,' " muttered Harrison. "Here goes!" He extricated himself from the car, in which they had all taken refuge as soon as the rain began, and climbed up one of the pillars.

"Come down, you fool!" hissed Waite; but Harrison, regardless of the fact that the light had not yet gone, and that he was easily visible, climbed on. The ascent, to one of his height and (when he chose, as he did now, to call upon it), his sinuous agility, was easy enough. The stone facings and orna-mentations of the porch were unexpectedly firm, considering their dilapi-dated appearance, and he was soon on top of the porch and crouching down to peer in at the broken window. Waite joined him, and they found them-selves staring into what seemed to be the library of the house. They peered and listened, but nothing could be either heard or seen.

"Come on," breathed Waite; and climbed in. Harrison gingerly followed, and they found themselves in a long, paneled gallery, snuff-brown with an-cient books. "You take that end and I'll take this one," said Waite. "I really think the house is empty, but if anybody comes, scoot like hell, and don't break your neck getting down."

It was soon clear that unless the diptych was hidden behind books (which, unfortunately for the seekers, was only too patent a possibility) it was not in the long gallery, for, except for the laden shelves and a table with two draw-ers, both of which proved to be empty, there was nowhere for it to be. Harri-son opened the door at his end of the gallery and passed out on to a landing. He descended the wooden staircase and found himself in what were obvi-ously the kitchen regions. He glanced round, and looked in the kitchen dresser, but as it seemed unlikely that the diptych would be there, he retraced his steps and passed along the gallery again to contact Waite and report his pre-liminary failure.

He could not find his friend at first, and did not like to call out. Then he met Waite in a small ante-room and hurriedly whispered his remarks. Waite nodded and switched off his torch.

"We're on the main staircase here," he murmured. "I'll go down, if you like, and you can do the rest of the rooms on this floor."

They crept through an archway to the front staircase, a fine affair in oak, carved with garlands. Waite, passing an appreciative hand over the topmost carving, descended to the entrance hall, and Harrison went on, across the top of the stairs and through another archway, into a vast bedroom. A brief search in the unlocked drawers of dressing-table, tall-boy and wardrobe convinced him that the diptych was not in any of them. He turned his attention to the great four-poster bed. It was unmade and had been slept in, but, although he searched it, and looked behind its hangings and on the floor, there was still no sign of what he sought.

He gave it up, and tiptoed down the stairs to join Waite. He found him in the entrance hall, and reported that the bedroom was evidently not the hiding place for the treasure.

"There's nothing on this floor, either," said Waite. "That means, I suppose, that we must take out all those damned books in the long gallery. Everywhere else in the house is as bare as your hand, and, by the look of them, I should say that most of the rooms have never been lived in, as that chap said."

"The bedroom had," said Harrison. "Look here, if we're really going to tackle those confounded books, we'd better get Peter in to help us. It's clear the house is empty. Let's tell him to park the car down the drive where it won't very easily be spotted if anybody *does* come along, and then get him to climb in as we did."

Waite considered this scheme, and then pronounced in its favor. He went to the broken window and softly whistled, but Piper, inside the car, did not hear him, so he climbed out, descended, and gave the new instructions. Piper, bored and chilly, embraced the changed plan with enthusiasm. The pair of them drove off, returned shortly, and Piper followed Waite up the heavily-ornamented porch. Harrison had news.

"I say," he said, as soon as they had joined him in the long gallery, "there's been some mistake. I was fiddling about with a whacking great desk in that small study on the ground floor. . . ."

"I'd already searched that," said Waite.

"Yes, but did you look at that pile of letters in the rack on top?"

"Just took the lot out and shoved them back. Obvious the diptych wasn't there." Waite sounded apologetic, but the ingenuous Harrison did not notice this.

"I know. Did you look at the envelopes?" he enquired.

"No. There wasn't any point."

"Wasn't there, though!" said Harrison, his voice breaking on a note of mirth. "They were all addressed to Havers, and at Merlin's *Castle!*"

"What!"

"Fact, I assure you. Every bally one. We've been and gone and cracked the wrong crib. Those fellows who directed us were perfectly sane. We were in the district of the Castle, not the Furlong, so they naturally concluded that it was the Castle we wanted!"

There was a second's pause whilst the other two struggled with their feelings.

"Talk about robbing Peter to pay Paul! We've been trying to rob Peter to pay Peter! Oh, let's get out of this, or I shall die of congested hysteria!" shouted Piper.

"The trouble is that the whole countryside seems to be called after Merlin," remarked Harrison. "Anyway, what do we do next?"

"Perfectly simple," said Waite, recovering his usual manner. "Let's have a look at these books. If I know old Havers, everything will be in some kind of orderly confusion. What we want is something topographical of about the early nineteenth century, I imagine. You know, something longwinded and high-flown which deals with the alleged history of the neighborhood. As David suggests, there must be two houses, both called Merlin's something. One is Merlin's Furlong, which is the one we're after, and the other is this one, Merlin's Castle. Well, the Furlong can't be very far away, and I think that if we can find a map or some directions in one of those topographical dust-traps we can do the job tonight as we'd planned."

"Agreed," said Piper. Harrison said that he was hungry.

"Yes," said Waite. "What about sticking old Havers for a meal? He can't object to that when we are giving up all this time and taking all this trouble on his behalf. You two go down and forage, whilst I inspect some of these tomes."

By the time Harrison and Piper had unearthed tinned food, some biscuits and a decanter half-full of port, he told them that he had found what he wanted. He produced a calf-bound volume and proceeded to read aloud from it.

"Thirteen miles?" repeated Piper, through a mouthful of Russian salad and cold baked beans. "Do it on our heads when we've finished this grub. Which direction from here?"

"Over the hill and straight on, apparently. It doesn't sound as though one can miss it. Gobble up, dears. We're going to have our bit of fun after all."

Only the morbid-minded, Cassandra-like Harrison was anxious to remain any longer in Merlin's Castle. He rinsed the plates under the scullery tap and left the empty tins stacked neatly upon the draining board, taking as long as he could in spite of the complaints of the others. Waite, in particular, grumbled, and stood between him and the door which led into an ancient coach-house adjacent to the stone-flagged scullery.

At last they returned to the car and drove away sedately, as though they were honored guests who had stayed rather late after dinner.

At the end of the weed-grown path, Piper, who had the wheel, turned to the left, drove uphill and followed the road, in spite of Waite's protests that he had missed the turning. At four miles they were ascending another long hill between high and ragged hedges which the headlamps turned into a jungle of black and green. Suddenly before them loomed the stern and dreadful fastness of Merlin's Fort.

"Well, I'm dashed! The other side of it!" cried Harrison. At crossroads a signpost informed them with incurious exactitude: MONOLITH 3¼. RUNT 2½. GATES 5¾. TO MERLIN'S FURLONG ONLY.

"Sort of crossroads where suicides used to be buried," said Piper. "I want to go home to my mum! Talk about the road to Merlin's Fort being unsuitable for motors! This one looks worse to me!"

"Yes, but, as I told you, you shouldn't have taken it," said Waite. For so phlegmatic a man he sounded agitated. The sensitive Harrison glanced at him, looked away, and made no remark.

"Funny about our mistake," said Piper chattily.

"Keep your eye on the road and look out for signposts," said Waite.

CHAPTER FIVE

Merlin's Jest

"Nor need you on mine honor, have to do
With any scruple."

SHAKESPEARE—*Measure for Measure*

That the road was unsuitable for motors was very soon apparent. Humps, bumps, dips and deep ruts presented such a bar to progress that at three miles an hour the car still seemed to be about to shed her back axle.

Suddenly the road stopped at a pair of double gates. These were shut fast, but were not locked, and the united efforts of Waite and Harrison (for Piper was still driving) at last contrived to separate them sufficiently to allow the car to pass through.

Unlike that at Merlin's Castle, this drive was a very short one, and less than fifty yards brought the car to an imposing fifteenth-century gatehouse. Its archway was unbarred, and, once through it, the three young men found themselves confronting the high twin towers of a castellated manor house whose wide front door, picked out by the headlights of the car, looked formidable and forbidding.

"Switch off," said Waite from the back seat behind the driver. Piper obliged, and the car remained in darkness and in silence. "No lights anywhere in the house," added Waite at last. "Come on. Let's go."

The entrance doors to Merlin's Furlong gave at a touch. Behind them was an archway containing two more doors, one on the right and one on the left of the entrance.

"All collegiate, so far," muttered Waite; and was justified in this assertion, for, shown by the light of torches discreetly shaded, it was soon evident that the archway debouched on to a quadrangle of considerable size around which were grouped the main buildings.

"So what?" demanded Harrison in a whisper.

"Separate, and seek an entrance," responded Waite. "And the devil take the hindmost. I'll try those doors to the towers."

"I vote we stick together," suggested Piper. "It's going to be sticky if one of us gets caught and the others don't know where he is."

This point of view was universally adopted, even the impatient Waite perceiving its value; so, cautiously, they tried the door of the tower on the right. It opened. Behind it was a flight of rough stone steps which, after a short, sharp, straight ascent, brought them to a very small stone landing and the threshold of a nail-studded wooden door. This had an iron handle which turned with a sound of heavy clanking, and admitted them to a turret chamber containing an ancient Tudor bed with appropriate, although moth-eaten, hangings, a large cupboard, two cane-seated chairs with the seats worn right through, and a small square of carpet fastened down with screws.

The rest of the tower was not more productive, but the staircase had become a spiral which seemed to go on for ever. On the fourth floor, Waite, who was in the lead, stepped out into the air and only just saved himself from being precipitated from a broken pinnacle to the ground.

"Nightmare Castle," he remarked as, unperturbed, he stepped back on to the top of the broken stone staircase. "I don't think there's much doing here. I suggest we leave the twin tower until the end, and concentrate upon the main buildings."

They descended, and crossed the quadrangle—more properly, Piper suggested, the courtyard. Opposite the gatehouse archway was the great banqueting hall, and this was approached by a flight of seven steps which led to another nail-studded door. This was immovable, so Waite led the way to the eastward. Here their torches disclosed curtained windows, but none was open.

"I think we've had it," said Harrison hopefully.

"Not by a long chalk," said Waite. But, after further cautious exploration, even his stout-hearted faith began to falter. The embattled towers, and (as Harrison observed), the gorgeous pinnacles, offered no means of entry whatever.

"We'll have to break something," said Waite.

"Let's try the tower again first," suggested Piper. "I spotted a little door in that Tudor bedroom. It might lead into a passage and connect with the house."

Somewhat dispiritedly his companions followed him. Waite did not believe that the little door would prove useful, for he thought that it would certainly be locked, and Harrison devoutly hoped it would be, but had an instinctive feeling it would not.

"Woe, woe," he muttered, for the small round-headed door burst open at Piper's strong push and disclosed a shallow recess which led to a passage, and the passage, in its turn, led to a suite of rooms on the north side of the courtyard. These rooms were furnished, and corresponded to the curtained suite which the young men had seen from outside.

"Now," said Waite, "we'd better separate. David, you go on as far as the end of this landing, and work back towards me. I'll begin here and work towards you. We must keep in touch. Peter, you go back to the car and make sure of our retreat. We may have to come out in a hurry. If anybody finds anything, or gets caught, yell like blazes. Surely both Merlin's Castle *and* Merlin's Furlong can't be completely uninhabited!"

Piper went down the stone staircase and back to the car, and the other two, stepping delicately, began their careful search for the purloined diptych. They met in the middle of the corridor at last, but with nothing to show for their trouble.

"That's that," said Waite, impatiently. "Oh, well, we must just carry on. I think I'll go on to the banqueting hall while you have a look at these rooms along this next corridor. Begin with this first one, and we'll work towards one another again."

"All right," agreed Harrison, much happier now that he felt certain the house was empty. But the house was not quite empty. He put his head in at the second doorway, listened for the sound of breathing, heard nothing, and switched on his torch. In ten seconds he was out in the corridor, stumbling along towards the banqueting hall.

"Polly! Polly!" he yelled. "Where are you?"

"Don't panic," said Waite, appearing at the end of the corridor. "What on earth's the matter?"

"Murder!" said Harrison. "I went into a bedroom, and the chap in there has had his head smashed in."

"Good Lord! That's torn it! Where?" They hurried along together.

"The second room I went into. What the devil shall we do? The house must be empty, except for—him!"

"We'd better make sure. Let's yell."

They shouted to such effect that there came a thunderous knocking from below.

"Ghosts of Macbeth and the porter!" muttered Harrison. "That'll be Peter, I trust. He heard us shout."

He went to the front door, but the bolts were rusted home and he could not budge them. He shouted, "Find the tower, Peter! This won't open!" Then he and Waite went back along the gallery to contact Piper at the top of the first flight of steps.

"What's up?" he asked when he had joined them. Harrison told him.

"Along here, and it's rather a mess," he said.

Sprawled across a four-poster bed was the dead body of a man. He was wearing a dressing-gown over ancient stovepipe black trousers. He was lying on his face, and even the color of his hair could scarcely be determined owing to the mess of dried blood which covered his skull.

The three young men stood in silence. Then Harrison asked:

"What shall we do? We'd better not touch him. I mean . . . there's not much doubt."

"No doubt at all," said Waite drily. "It means the police, of course, and then we *are* in a jam."

"Two of us had better stay here while the third one goes," suggested Piper.

"You go, then," said Waite. "You look an innocent sort of bloke, which I don't, and it would really be better for David not to go, as he found the body. The police always suspect the first person who gives information of a murder."

Piper stood staring at the body. He asked, "How long, do you think. . . ?"

"I don't know. Not since *we've* been in the house. The blood is quite dry, not just coagulated. Pop off, then, and do your best. Gentlemanly bewilderment, but otherwise the truth, I suggest. "I cannot tell a lie, father. It was the cat." That's the line to take, I rather fancy." Waite's tone was light, but he talked through his teeth.

"I'll do what I can," said Piper. "Where will you be when I get back?"

"In the bedroom with this. It will look more natural, as we claim to be innocent parties. We were out on a toot, remember, and intended nothing but a rag. And *don't* mention we made a mistake and went to Merlin's Castle."

"Right. So long, then." He went off, and the other two walked out of the dead man's room to the top of the stairs, where, from a window they opened, they could hear the car drive away.

"Now what?" asked Harrison. "Because this is going to be sticky. Whatever tale Peter tells, we're in the soup. And, anyway, who *is* the dead bloke?"

"I don't know any more than you do. But I've got a nasty feeling that it's old Aumbry, whom Havers wanted to kill. Anyway, whoever he is, I agree there's bound to be a stink. After all, we *did* break in, and we did intend to get the diptych. And, by the powers," he added suddenly, "I'm hanged if I don't have another look for it! It will be something to do while Peter's gone. I'm not going back into that bedroom until I hear the police."

Harrison attempted to dissuade him, and suddenly broke off thankfully to say:

"Anyway, you're too late! I can hear the car, I think."

"I shouldn't have thought Peter would get back as soon as this," objected Waite.

They continued to listen.

"That's not our car," said Harrison.

"No, I don't believe it is, but it's just possible it's the police. Peter may have met them along the road."

"Well, how are they going to get in?"

"We'd better let them in, I suppose."

"But we told Peter we'd stay in the bedroom."

"Oh, dear! Yes, so we did. Hang on a bit, I suggest, and see what happens."

What happened was very curious. A window by the side of which they were standing overlooked the interior of the gate-house arch. A car shot underneath the arch, but instead of stopping at the front entrance it drove on round the courtyard.

"Quick! That first corridor! The one from the tower," said Waite. "Take the first room and I'll take the second. We'll see pretty well from there." But they were not quite quick enough. Slight noises, and the sound of a door being opened, indicated that the new arrival . . . there seemed only one set of footsteps . . . had made entrance by means of a latchkey.

"What do we do now?" whispered Harrison.

"See where he goes and what he does," returned Waite. "They say the murderer always returns to the scene of the crime, and two of us can account for him if he's nasty. I'd like to know what all this is about. Besides . . ." He did not need to finish. It would be as well, as Harrison could plainly see, that they should not be the only persons on the premises when the police turned up.

"In fact," he murmured, "how would it be if we nabbed him?"

"No," Waite whispered back, "too dangerous for *us* if he turns out to be a perfectly harmless bloke with legitimate business here."

"How can he have, sneaking in like this after midnight?"

"Keep quiet. We'll try to get a glimpse of him if he puts on a light."

But it was soon clear that, like themselves, the newcomer was not prepared to switch on lights. He did not even use an electric torch. He turned into one of the rooms at the opposite end of the corridor, and they could hear his squeaking shoes as he moved about.

"I'd give anything to know what he's doing," whispered Waite. "I'm going to find out."

He removed his shoes and sneaked out of the room in which they were hiding, but his stockinged feet slipped on the floorboards and he fell full length. The noise apparently frightened the stranger considerably. He gave a yelp of terror, and the next moment he was running away from Waite, who picked himself up and went in pursuit. But again the treacherous floorboards laid him low, and Harrison, hastening after him, fell over him. A door slammed somewhere, and, by the time they had gained a window which overlooked the courtyard, the unknown man was in his car and all they saw was the rear lamp as he drove off under the gatehouse archway.

"I suppose we've done a rather daft thing," said Harrison. "We should have gone off with Peter, and telephoned the police first thing in the morning."

"Better to stick it out. They'd have found us in the end, and then we should have looked pretty silly. The way things are already will look bad enough, I know, but to be picked up on the run, so to speak, would be incredibly worse. I'll tell you what, though. As soon as we know what's going to happen to us we'll contact Bradley of Angelus."

"His aunt, you mean."

"Of course. Thank God I invited him to my last party and made him play his violin. These musicians are a choosy lot, but I lushed him up and only had serious people who, I felt, would really listen. He's good, you know."

"His aunt will have to be good, too, if she's to get us out of this jam," said Harrison sadly. "The least *I* can hope for is a sentence for manslaughter. They're certain to say the man surprised me and I hit him on the head in a panic. I do panic, you know."

"I hadn't noticed." But Waite was dispirited, too.

"I'm panicking now," said Harrison, "because I'm sure I can hear the sound of a car, and this time it's bound to be the police."

This forecast turned out to be correct. Piper had come back accompanied by an alert sergeant, a constable and a doctor.

"And now, sir," said the sergeant, looking at Waite.

Waite shrugged. "You'd better take a statement," he said. "I got these men into this by way of a rag, and it hasn't turned out too well. My name is . . ."

CHAPTER SIX

Merlin's Myrmidons

"We can nor lost friends nor sought foes recover,
But, meteor-like, save that we move not, hover."

John Donne—Calm

It was apparent to the Chief Constable that the inspector was worried and anxious.

"I know they didn't do it, sir," he insisted. "And yet, if they didn't, who did? Gentlemen of their age and standing are wild. A good thing they are, in a way, but there's no doubt they'd made up their minds to get hold of this diptych and return it to Professor Havers. I know these sort of sparks, sir. Once they'd made up their minds they'd go to all lengths to carry out their intentions. Well, all lengths short of murder, that's to say. And yet two murders have happened. What's the answer?"

"*Two* murders?" The Chief Constable looked mildly surprised.

"Well, yes, I'm afraid so, sir. You see, we held on to our three young gentlemen last night, and then one of them, a certain Mr. Waite, seemed to crack up a bit and suddenly told me that they'd decided to get back this diptych belonging to Professor Havers. They'd missed their way to Merlin's Furlong, which, to us that know the countryside, isn't surprising, and landed themselves up at Professor Havers's own place, Merlin's Castle. They didn't know it, but the professor's dead body was lying in the coach-house, out beyond the scullery and the woodshed. My sergeant saw it this morning.

"Now, sir, we know quite a lot about Professor Havers, and none of it does him much credit. He appears to have been a clever sort of old gentleman up to the winter of 1944, when the war seems to have got on his nerves and he took to all sorts of funny doings in order to occupy his mind. He never actually ran foul of the law, but there was a fussation at a certain university of which he was, and still is, a member, and he was asked to vacate his rooms in college and give some sort of undertaking that he'd let up on some of his ideas. Then came the unexplained suicide of a certain young Mr. Catfield, a boy of twenty, found dead at Wallchester last year. You probably remember the case, sir?"

"Yes, of course. Very nasty business."

"The floor of the coach-house where the professor's body was found is of stone, and all sorts of queer-shaped figures and designs seem to have been scrawled over it with red and white chalk. Looks as if there were certain ideas the professor hadn't given up, after all, sir, if you understand me."

"Yes, yes, Ekkers. But what about the body itself?"

"Hit over the head, sir, same as the late Mr. Aumbry that these boys found and reported."

"And you sent the sergeant over to Merlin's Castle because this young Waite confessed that they'd been there?"

"Yes, that's it, sir. Pure matter of routine. No idea we should find another body."

"Fingerprints?"

"The young gentlemen made no objection, sir, although I told them they were at liberty to refuse to have them taken. Doesn't help us at all. Their prints were all over the rooms where they admitted they'd looked for the diptych, but not in the coach-house."

"A good thing for them they confessed. Very awkward indeed if we'd found out later on that they'd been inside Merlin's Castle, and hadn't thought fit to mention it."

"Yes, sir. A very curious coincidence that there was a dead man in the Castle and another in the Furlong."

"Very curious indeed. All the same, the young idiots seem to have acted as sensibly as could be expected. What's the next step, apart from the inquests? By the way, do those fellows know that a body has been found at Merlin's Castle?"

"No, sir. Naturally I thought I should tell you first."

"Well, look here, confront them suddenly with the fact and note their reactions. I don't suppose it will help, but you never know. Is there anybody among Professor Havers' acquaintance who. . . ?"

"We don't know yet, sir. He did keep two Negro servants, and one of them seems to have been in trouble. But, I think, if you don't mind, sir, I'll have another go at the youngsters. Something else might break. You never know."

"Yes, I can quite see, from what we said last night, that it all looks pretty fishy to you," said Waite, "but I really think . . . you know, Boat Race Night and all that . . . possibly we can explain it."

He began to explain it, but was stopped at once by the inspector, who said heavily but in indulgent tones, "Perhaps one at a time, sir, in private, like. You first, sir."

"You'll find we shall all tell the same story, just as I expect we did last night, but, of course, as you please," said Waite, when he had been escorted into another room. "It was my idea in the first place that we should indulge in this rag, but that's all it was . . . a rag, and just a bit of bad luck at the end of it."

He again gave the gist of their adventures, and emphasized that they had already climbed into Merlin's Castle under the mistaken impression that it was Merlin's Furlong, but he amended this confession by adding that the window above the porch had already been broken before their arrival.

"And exactly what is this diptych you gentlemen are supposed to be looking for?" enquired the inspector, turning over the page of his notebook.

"Well, it's a . . . Look here, suppose your notebook had only the covers and no inside pages, and suppose that inside each cover was a valuable picture, or a sort of carving, maybe, and the covers were of wood or ivory or metal, well, that would be a diptych."

"How big would it be, sir?"

"Oh, almost any size. They come in a matter of a few square inches, or you could have one big enough to form the reredos in a church."

"And how big was this one belonging, it is alleged, to Professor Havers? That's my question, sir."

"Look here, less of the "it is alleged." If Professor Havers said he had a diptych and that it had been stolen, I should believe him."

"Very good, sir. And what size would it have been?"

"Well, it sounds a bit silly, now you ask me, but, as a matter of absolute fact, we forgot to ask, don't you know."

"A curious lapse, sir, wasn't it, when you were all set to get it back. How would you know what to look for?"

Piper and Harrison did not fare much better. The inspector, although comparatively unlettered, was shrewd.

"This urge, sir, to which you refer," he said to Harrison. "Had you ever experienced the same sort of urge before?"

"Look here," said Harrison, "I can't say any more, and I don't want a lawyer. What we want is to get in touch with Bradley of Angelus."

"And you think this gentleman can help you, sir?"

"No, but his aunt might. Yes, and talking of aunts, we should have been down this way a good deal sooner and perhaps not been mixed up in all this if it hadn't been for gate-crashing Waite's aunt."

"How do you mean, sir?" The inspector, who had already sent a policeman with an urgent message to the Chief Constable, was anxious to present his superior with as much more detail as possible but felt that this intrusion of aunts was unfortunate. Waite, challenged, took up the story and explained. He suggested that the inspector might like to call up his aunt, whose telephone number he gave, in support of Harrison's allegations. The inspector smiled.

"It wouldn't help either you or ourselves, sir. You see, whether it was accident or intention that caused you to visit your aunt and stay there all that time neither you nor we can prove."

"You can ask my aunt. She'll tell you she had no knowledge that we should call on her."

"Quite so, sir, but she can't tell me, without any doubts, that *you* didn't know you were going to."

"Oh, I see. I suppose, as you say it was Mr. Aumbry, who'd taken the diptych, lying dead there, it looks pretty bad for us now we've let you know our intention of getting it back for Professor Havers." Waite sounded incoherent.

"Gentlemen," said the inspector solemnly, when he had all three together again, "the very fact that you all told us your intention of getting back the diptych (when you must have had a pretty shrewd idea that the dead man *was* Mr. Aumbry) was the most sensible thing you could have done. In fact, I don't mind telling you. . . ." He picked up the telephone which was yelling like a noisy infant. "Excuse me a minute. Yes. Yes? Very good, Sergeant. As soon as the Chief arrives I'll be right along. You know what to do. You'll want the photographer and the fingerprint people. Yes, it does look funny! You're telling *me*!" He put the receiver down. The Chief Constable had just rung up to tell him to drop his bomb.

"You were saying?" suggested Waite courteously. The inspector eyed him.

"I shall have to hold on to you gentlemen for a bit, I'm thinking," he said. "Something very, very unforeseen has happened. I'll have to see what the Chief's got to say. Meanwhile, I'll have to ask you to stay here. It's all irregular, but I'm blessed if I see what else to do."

"Nonsense," said Waite boldly. "You've got nothing on us that the local beaks can't settle. You jolly well bring us up in front of the justices, or I'll sue you for wrongful arrest."

"I haven't arrested you, not yet, sir," the inspector mildly stated, "but you'll realize I'm in a proper fix. You confessed you'd been in Merlin's Castle last night as well as in Merlin's Furlong, didn't you? Well, that phone message was from my sergeant. As you said you'd been over to Merlin's Castle I sent him over there just to check your story and have a general look round, and I'm afraid he's gone and found another body."

The Chief Constable shook his head.

"It's difficult, very difficult, Ekkers. Let's go over the evidence once again and then I'll have these three young fools in front of me and talk to them like a Dutch uncle."

"Yes, sir?"

"Then we'll let them go, having charged them to keep their mouths shut, which, for their own sakes as well as ours, I hope they will. We can't hold them indefinitely without charging them, and if we arrest them for house-

breaking or illegal entry or something, the fat will be in the fire once the
news of these murders gets out. Besides, we've only their word that they
ever broke into these houses. The papers haven't got hold of anything yet,
and if we can insist on an undertaking from these fellows that they won't go
blabbing their heads off to the reporters when the thing *does* break. . . ."

"There's the inquest, sir. They'll have to give evidence as to the finding of
the body of Mr. Aumbry."

"Only young Harrison need do that, of course, but there's a snag if the
coroner is permitted to ask him what he was doing there. Perhaps that point
need not arise. The inquest must, in any case, be adjourned, so it shouldn't
be difficult to tip the coroner the wink that the police have something up
their sleeves which they are not yet prepared to disclose. Let him hear Harrison, the medical evidence and a short report from you, and that will be all.
I'm as convinced of the innocence of these ridiculous chaps as you are. Of
course, it won't hurt to keep the tabs on them in a quiet and unobtrusive
manner. There's one thing in favor of their silly exploit, though. At least they
brought us on to the scene of both murders days sooner than we might have
heard of them, and, in a case of this kind, that may prove very important.
Well, let's go through the thing again. One never knows. Something else
may emerge."

"Very good, sir, although there's precious little to go on. It began last
Monday afternoon at Mr. Piper's home, when they found a curiously
worded advertisement which I've checked. Their report of it is accurate.
They seem to have concluded that Professor Havers, who, as I reminded
you, according to some confidential reports I've got, was a gentleman of
peculiar fancies . . ."

"What sort of peculiar fancies? You mentioned those drawings on the coach-
house floor, and, of course, I know . . ."

"Here are the reports, sir. I had to take them down over the phone, but I'm
sure they're exact. They add up to what we both know, but are a bit more
detailed."

"Hm! Yes. *Peculiar* is the word. Has the body at Merlin's Castle been
identified officially?"

"Well, sir, not officially, although we know quite well it's the professor. I
got a description of him from our three young sparks, too. I wondered if . . ."

"Good idea. Take them along to have a look at it . . . the corpse. Interesting
to note their reactions. Show them in one at a time, of course. Then you'd
better get hold of his landlady to make absolutely sure. Did you get her
address? . . . Oh, yes, I see. It's here in the report. She might be able to help
us in other ways, too."

"I doubt it, sir. Very cagey, these landladies, about their guests. It might
pay her, in a way, to keep her mouth shut."

"Agreed. But we must tackle her, none the less. Anything else to go on?"

"Nothing very helpful, sir, I'm afraid. The Wallchester police said something about a doll, but I couldn't make any sense out of what they told me. It seems that young Piper, or one of them, handed this doll to a constable who took it to his headquarters and handed it in."

"A doll, eh? A magic doll, I suppose. Did you question these youngsters about it?"

"Yes, sir. They were ribald."

"Oh, *were* they?"

"Yes, sir." The inspector smiled indulgently. "Young gentlemen of their caliber will have their little jokes. There's not a ha'porth of harm in any of them. On that I'd take my oath."

"Yes. Well, look here, before you go to Wallchester and tackle the landlady, let's just have the time-scheme over again. I don't want to miss any pointer, however slight."

"Very good, sir. Here it is. By Wednesday morning our three gentlemen were in Wallchester, Mr. Piper and Mr. Harrison informing the professor that they would help him. I asked them whether he knew who they were, but they declare that they don't really think he did. That I find hard to believe, sir, because they admit that, at one time and another, they've all attended his lectures."

"What did he lecture on? Do we know? Although I don't suppose it's important."

The inspector consulted his notebook very respectfully this time, and gave a slight cough before he answered.

"The Theory and Practice of Palace Accounts as kept by the Merovingian Court Officials, with special reference to the Effect on French Foreign Policy and the Power of the Papacy, sir," he at length replied.

"Good heavens! All that?"

"Yes, sir."

"Odd! Still, it gives us one pointer. He may not have known them . . . these three undergraduates, I mean. I shouldn't think they would have attended many lectures on a subject like that."

"Mr. Waite said that the lectures were illuminating and instructive, sir."

"No doubt he did. Doesn't necessarily mean *he* found them so. All right, Ekkers, go on. On Wednesday morning they were briefed . . ."

"Receiving this doll from the professor, sir, which they presented to Constable Fewer of the Wallchester police . . ."

"And . . . by the way, what had happened to them on Tuesday? We haven't gone into that yet."

"They went to the *Granville* in Wallchester High Street, where they had dinner and stayed the night. Well, that's their story."

"Is it confirmed in any way?"

"Yes, sir. The office staff and the waiters know them well, and say that they were there and had breakfast and lunch next day, which would be the Wednesday."

"Oh, yes. What did they do for the rest of Wednesday, I wonder?"

"Went back to Mr. Piper's house, sir, according to themselves, and set out after dinner for Merlin's Furlong . . . only they got it mixed up with Merlin's Castle, at which they eventually arrived."

"But they didn't get *there* until Friday! What happened between Wednesday and Friday?"

"That's what needs some explaining. According to them, they broke their journey to drop a note in on the professor to tell him they'd started off to get back the diptych, and then they broke the journey again to spend the night at Mr. Waite's aunt's."

"And she wasn't expecting them."

"No, sir. She gave them some food and found them somewhere to sleep, and they say they lunched in Moundbury here at midday on Thursday."

"Confirmed?"

"Oh, yes, sir. We've had the aunt on the phone. She swears to them, and the head-waiter at the Bell here remembered them perfectly. So did the hall porter and the waiter at the Bell, where they returned for Thursday dinner, having lost the way to Merlin's Furlong. They spent Thursday night in their car, having lost the way once again, and they went back for Friday breakfast. They remained for lunch, and at last got to Merlin's Castle. However, they were then under the impression, according to them, that it was Merlin's Furlong, where they expected to find the diptych."

"Any confirmation that they spent Thursday night in their car?"

"No, I'm afraid there isn't, sir, not so far, but we have hopes of tracing a man that they spoke to early on Friday morning."

"On this evidence they *could* have killed Professor Havers, then?"

"But I'm certain they did nothing of the sort, sir."

"Yes, I know, but it's very, very tiresome. Damn the young idiots! Two murders, and they were on the premises in each case! It really doesn't give us a chance. If they were on the loose, and unaccounted for, on Thursday night, we can't ignore the fact. This business of Thursday night puts a different complexion on things. Well, have them in. They may be able to think of some way of getting themselves out of this jam. I'd like to hear again what they've got to say. And you'd better get that doll of the professor's from the people at Wallchester. There might be something about it that would help. Dolls are among the wickedest things on earth! If Professor Havers was messing about with dolls he may have been up to anything—especially judging from what we know of him already."

"And may have annoyed somebody, sir?" The inspector's tone was courteous rather than convinced.

"Difficult to say, but one thing I do know. Where there's magic there's mischief. I was in Paris once . . . Well, never mind that now!"

"You know, sir, in the case of Mr. Aumbry, there is another line of investigation."

"I know. Seems to have had some nephews, according to those acceptances of invitations your chaps found in Aumbry's desk. Gives us their addresses, too. One of them may have had some good motive for killing his uncle. The only trouble is that the two murders might be connected, and I really don't see why these nephews would have wanted Professor Havers out of the way. I'm certain there must be a factor in the case which hasn't yet come to light. Oh, well, hang those young idiots! No, I don't mean it literally! Anyway, let's see what we can get out of them now they've had a little more time to think things over."

"I fancy they've told the truth, sir . . . or as much of it as they know."

"Very likely." The Chief Constable grinned. "Nobody would ever think you'd been a schoolboy!"

(2)

"The whole thing was simply a rag," said Waite doggedly. "Admittedly it was silly and a bit risky, but that's absolutely all it was. We read Professor Havers' advertisement and went to answer it. He gave us the doll and the . . . er . . ."

"His blessing," put in Harrison helpfully.

". . . and that's all there was to it."

"The police suggest," said the Chief Constable in a heavy, official voice, "that you were surprised while you were rummaging round for this diptych, and that you struck Mr. Aumbry down in a moment of panic. If you plead to that in court, the verdict is bound to be manslaughter, not, of course, murder, as no evil intention is foreshadowed or would be envisaged by the law."

"Panic be blowed!" said Piper. "We found Mr. Aumbry's body, and had no idea at the time that Professor Havers was also dead. I think the police ought to recognize the fact that we reported to them at once. Dash it, we could have made off, and you'd never have known we'd been there. I admit that our fingerprints are all over everything, but they're not on record and wouldn't have helped you."

"As a matter of fact, sir, you're right there," put in the inspector, "and it's a point in your favor. On the other hand, once we'd found the two bodies it would have been only a matter of time before we tracked you down."

"Baloney!" said Waite rudely. The inspector looked at him with an indulgent eye.

"I assure you, sir," he said mildly.

"Well, what else do you want to know, sir?" asked Harrison, addressing the Chief Constable. "And when you've told us," he added suddenly, on a disarming and youthful note, "we want to get in touch with a man called Bradley."

"Wait a minute," said Piper. "On this question of tracking us down. Why should you have thought of such a thing?"

"Constable Fewer, of the Wallchester police, saw you with the doll," said the Chief Constable. "In fact, we know you gave it him."

"Even so . . ."

"No, no, my dear chap. Magic . . . that is to say, *black* magic . . . is known all over the world, and the rituals are astonishingly alike. You may not realize it, but the history of these evil dolls has been investigated in North and South America, in France, the South Sea Islands, the West Indies, Italy, and even (and I'm referring to comparatively modern times) in England. All over Africa magic dolls are known and feared. You took a big risk when you accepted one from Professor Havers, upon whom, I don't mind telling you, the Wallchester police have kept a discreet, but official, eye for quite a time. Knowing this, Constable Fewer was not satisfied that the doll was an innocent toy. He handed it in as obscene."

"Oh, rot!" exclaimed Piper. "A doll's a doll, and a rag's a rag, and nothing will persuade me differently."

"It's no good, Peter," said Harrison. "It's not really the doll that matters. It's some connection between old Havers and Mr. Aumbry that has sunk us."

"I'm glad you realize it, sir," said the inspector.

"One thing I'd like to know," said Harrison, "and that is where you found the body. I mean, we did rather look into things because of thinking we were at Merlin's Furlong and wanting to find the diptych."

"All in good time, sir," said the inspector, "if you'd kindly all come along."

Accompanied by the three young men, he went out to his car. A second and a third car drew up, each with a policeman at the wheel. Waite was taken into the inspector's car, and the other two were also separated, and did not encounter one another again until each had seen the body.

"Where *did* you find him?" asked Waite on the journey back when each of the undergraduates had identified the body as that of Professor Havers.

"In the old coach-house, sir."

"Coach-house? We didn't see one."

"No, sir? It is a windowless building near to the woodshed. It is lighted by a large square of glass in its roof. The gentleman must have been killed instantaneously with a single smashing blow on the left temple. The body was lying beneath this big skylight and was spread-eagled on the stone floor. There is no doubt whatever that the gentleman was murdered."

"Well, the other one certainly was. I never saw such a hideous mess as the back of his head. But, look, you haven't answered our question," put in Harrison.

"Which one would that be, sir?"

"We want to get in touch with a certain Bradley of Angelus. Is that possible?"

"Certainly, sir. I am going into Wallchester to procure Professor Havers' doll. I can give Mr. Bradley any message you wish."

"But he won't be there. It's the Long Vacation."

"So it is, sir. Do you know his holiday address?"

"No, of course not. You'll have to find him for us."

"I could hardly undertake to do that, sir."

"Well, could you find his aunt?"

"I don't understand, sir. What could you require of his aunt?"

"Life, liberty and the pursuit of happiness. Look here, Inspector, have a heart! We're in a pretty filthy jam and you know it. Could you dig up Bradley's cousin, the Q.C., if you can't get hold of Bradley or the aunt?"

"I've never heard of him, sir."

"Dash it, of course you have! He's Sir Ferdinand Lestrange," said Waite.

"And he is this Mr. Bradley's cousin, sir?"

"I think so. Some sort of relative, anyhow. But the person we really want is the aunt, Mrs. Lestrange Bradley," said Harrison.

"Mrs. Lestrange Bradley, sir? Oh, we know all about *her* and could readily put you in touch. But never forget, sir," . . . he chuckled . . . "who sups with the devil will need a long spoon! It's of no use for you to think you can pull the wool over that particular lady's eyes!"

"I call that a very unkind remark, Inspector. We've told the truth, the whole truth (I think) and certainly nothing but the truth, all the way through, and we shall continue to do so."

"The only sensible policy, sir."

"And now, are you jugging us and bringing us before the beaks?"

"No, sir. So long as you gentlemen will agree to place yourselves at the disposal of the police, there is no reason for anything further just at present."

"Hm! I don't know that I care about that particularly guarded statement. Have we to stay in this neighborhood?"

"Not necessarily, sir. It is sufficient that we know where you are, so that we can get in touch with you upon matters arising."

"I see. Well, we'd better stick around until we've seen Mrs. Bradley. No doubt she'll want to see the spot marked X and so forth."

"Undoubtedly, sir. And there will be the inquest, of course, on Professor

Havers. We shall have to take your evidence of identity there."

"Oh, yes."

"It's odd, you know, sir," the inspector went on in less official tones, "about these two murders. That diptych you gentlemen thought fit to look for seems responsible, somehow. Just how valuable was it? Have you any idea?"

Piper again described the diptych according to the remarks which Professor Havers had made. The inspector was undoubtedly impressed.

"And you didn't come across any trace of it either at Merlin's Castle or Merlin's Furlong, sir?"

"Not a smell."

"A collector's piece, and of big money value as well," said the inspector thoughtfully. "Mark my words, sir, murder has been done for much less. Very unscrupulous, some of these private collectors."

"Well, old Aumbry must have been fairly unscrupulous to have pinched the thing from Havers in the first place," observed Piper.

"If he did such a thing, sir. We must bear in mind that you had only the professor's word for that. You've no proof whatever that he was the rightful owner of the diptych. And if I may say so, sir, that is where you gentlemen acted with lack of caution."

"Good Lord!" said Piper. "It never occurred to us that he wasn't telling the truth! Oh, dash it, I'm positively certain he was! What do *you* say, David?"

"Very likely he was, sir. I'm just saying that his word on the matter wasn't proof."

The Chief Constable and the inspector went into another huddle after the three young men had been dismissed.

"We've now checked up on everything we can, sir," the inspector announced.

"Oh? And what have we got?"

"Only that, according to the medical evidence, Professor Havers was killed on the Thursday night, most probably twenty-four hours before the young men arrived, and Mr. Aumbry had been dead a good bit longer . . . on the Wednesday night, the doctor says, or very early Thursday morning."

"Well, it's clear that those boys could have had nothing to do with the murder of Aumbry, but unfortunately any one of the three . . . or all of them, for that matter, or Waite and Piper, who elected to separate themselves from Harrison that night and sleep in the heather . . . could have reached Professor Havers' castle from Merlin's Fort and got back in time to appear to have established an alibi."

"Quite so, sir. The next line of approach seems to be to contact the Aumbry nephews and the personal servants of Professor Havers, and see what they can tell us. I don't know what to think about the murder of the professor, sir, but it does seem a good bit more likely, on the face of it, that his nephews would have had a stronger motive for wanting Mr. Aumbry out of the way than these young fellows would. Say what you like, sir, but young university gentlemen don't usually panic and start hitting elderly gentlemen over the head. It isn't their line."

"Yes, yes, I agree," said the Chief Constable. "Very true, of course. Now, the professor's personal servants at his lodgings were a Negro maid and a mulatto valet, weren't they? I wonder how the landlady liked them?"

"Very prejudiced, sir, apparently, although only the maid lived there."

"Were these servants married to one another?"

"Affianced, I understand, sir. The man had been in Professor Havers' employment a couple of years. I don't know about the girl, but I believe they went there together."

"Where had he been before that?"

"It seems he was in Liverpool, sir, and struck into a little bit of trouble."

"It's a far cry from Liverpool to Wallchester, and I don't mean the distance, Ekkers. What brought him there, I wonder?"

"It appears he wanted to better his education, sir. He thought he might obtain employment as a scout at one of the colleges, and so pick up some bits of learning."

"Poor devil!"

"Yes, sir."

"So the two servants were engaged to be married, were they? And Havers was, as we said before, a man of peculiar interests, not many of them of a very reputable kind. It seems to me that it might be worthwhile to make a special enquiry. He may have upset the girl (or perhaps annoyed her boy-friend) by being familiar or something. Quite staggering how indiscreet some elderly gentlemen can be."

"Downright nasty, too, sir. Yes, there might be a pointer there. I'll get on to it right away. One other thing, too, sir, occurs to me, talking of servants, and the professor having these two colored people. A great rambling house such as Merlin's Castle *must* have had servants to keep it in order. Where are they? We've not had anyone come forward, and, except for this mysterious stranger who came in with a latchkey while Mr. Waite and Mr. Harrison were waiting for Mr. Piper to bring us on to the scene, they don't appear to have found anyone in Merlin's Furlong either, except the body."

"We'll have to dig into all that. As you say, there must have been servants in both those houses. All the same, with regard to Professor Havers, as he lived in his city lodgings so much of the time, it's quite possible that the service at Merlin's Castle was casual labor from the village. If so, that may not help us very much. Merlin's Furlong is perhaps a different matter."

"Well, I don't know," said the inspector. "Seems to me, sir, we might as well get on to this Mrs. Bradley the three boys want to contact."

"But I know Mrs. Bradley. She might even prove them guilty, you know."

"If she proved Mr. Waite was guilty, I'm not so sure I'd disagree with her, sir."

"Waite? Oh, I don't know. A small man like that," said the Chief Constable, who stood six feet two in his socks. The inspector wagged a sage head.

"The littler the worser, sir, and he's very stocky," he said, "but I expect you're right. It's hardly sensible to suspect any one of the young gentlemen more than another. Shall I then get hold of Mrs. Bradley, sir?"

"Yes, Ekkers, and the sooner the better."

CHAPTER SEVEN

Merlin's Aunt

"We must not make a scarecrow of the law."

SHAKESPEARE—*Measure for Measure*

Mrs. Beatrice Adela Lestrange Bradley, whose sympathy was always with the young and whose sense of humor usually acted as an antidote to this unnecessarily sentimental attitude, arrived in Moundbury three hours after she had received the Chief Constable's telephone call, for the Chief Constable had thought it well that he, and not the inspector, should be the person to contact her.

He had outlined the case very cautiously, but had given her sufficient information without betraying any bias whatever. The undergraduates hailed her with genuine, although decently-concealed, relief.

"Not the *Three Musketeers,* or even the three witches, I'm afraid," said Harrison.

"And not *Three Men in a Boat,* but merely three men in the soup," Mrs. Bradley observed. "These seem very comfortable lodgings."

She and the undergraduates were in the inspector's wife's sitting room. It looked out on to rising ground beyond the neat front garden, and was well and tastefully furnished. Waite glanced round appreciatively.

"Yes," he said. "We ought to be incarcerated in the local jail, I suppose, but, of course, the police realize perfectly well that we don't know anything about the murders. What did you think of the inquest?"

"I did not think there was anything to think about it."

"No. The police are still pushing along with their enquiries, so they weren't giving anything away."

"Well, I hope *you're* going to give something away," said Mrs. Bradley. "I want you to tell me the whole story just as things happened."

Piper groaned and Harrison looked reproachful. Waite said, apologizing for these reactions:

"We've told it to the inspector, the Chief Constable, my uncle, Peter's father, David's guardian, and all three family lawyers. It's becoming rather stale, flat and unprofitable by now. Must you really have it?"

"I can't help you if I don't know all the facts. I've had them from the Chief Constable, it is true, but I prefer to hear first-hand evidence."

"Of course you do. Here, David, you begin, and Peter and I will add, contradict and, generally speaking, interrupt. Nothing must be left out, put in or exaggerated."

Harrison gave a concise but detailed account of their adventures, beginning with the newspaper advertisement and ending with their report to the police that they had discovered Aumbry's body. At her request he quoted the advertisement *verbatim.*

"At what time did you get to Mr. Aumbry's house?" Mrs. Bradley demanded.

"Towards midnight, I should say. But we messed about in the tower for a bit, so we didn't discover straight away that Mr. Aumbry had been killed. I can't see why the police haven't jugged us. I mean, we don't seem able to *show* that we didn't get to Merlin's Furlong until about midnight on Friday. So far as the police are concerned, we'd been hanging about in the neighborhood since the midday of Thursday."

"But Mr. Aumbry, according to the medical evidence given at the inquest, died at some time between midnight and three on Wednesday–Thursday," put in Waite. "That ought to count in our favor so far as Merlin's Furlong is concerned, but Professor Havers was killed at a time which could be decidedly awkward for us if the police chose to look at it that way."

"Oh, yes, we *could* have killed Havers quite easily," agreed Harrison. "There's no reason, so far as the time-limits are concerned, why we did not. Only . . . we didn't, and we haven't the faintest idea who did. The police do really believe us. There's not much doubt about that. On the other hand, except for us, there isn't a suspect in sight."

"You've mentioned to the police, of course, this manservant to whom you gave a lift in your car to the station?"

"As a matter of fact we haven't. We've talked it over, but I'm sure he's as innocent as we are. If he were guilty, he'd hardly have acted as he did, and we can't let him in for all this." Waite waved his arm in explanation.

"Besides, he couldn't have killed Aumbry?" suggested Harrison.

"How do you know that?" Mrs. Bradley demanded. "Now, let's see. You gave this man a lift to the station from Merlin's Castle on Friday at . . ."

"About half-past two, I think. It couldn't have been earlier, but I shouldn't think it was very much later," said Piper.

"Are you sure he caught a train?"

"No. We left him at the booking hall. He went inside, to the ticket office . . . well, I suppose it was to the ticket office. . . ."

"And he had told you that Merlin's Castle was up for sale. Now, the police must be told about this man. If *you* don't tell them, I shall take it upon myself to do so."

"But won't it look odd that we've kept it dark?" argued Harrison. Mrs.

Bradley looked at him compassionately but with a glint of humor behind her pity.

"You seem to have behaved extremely oddly all the way through," she said. "After all, every night isn't Boat Race Night, you know."

The young men groaned, and Piper beat his breast.

"Puts her finger unerringly upon the spot," he proclaimed. "That's what Bradley said about her, and he was right."

"I think," said Mrs. Bradley, who loved the young and detested seeing them in difficulties of their own making, "that I had better hint to the Chief Constable, who can then pitch the tale to the inspector, that it was only by dint of the most rigid and brilliant cross-questioning on my part that this information about the manservant was brought to light; in short, that you had forgotten that the man existed. But I certainly think his activities must be investigated. The long and short of it is that, whether he knew it or not, his employer was already dead when he left the house on Friday afternoon. Then there is the matter of the women servants. The man, you say, referred to a cook and a couple of maids, yet, when you entered the house, the place was empty. What did you gather from this fact?"

"Board wages, I suppose," said Waite.

"The manservant gave no such indication, did he?"

"No. But we weren't with him very long. It was only about a couple of miles to the station."

"Now about Merlin's Furlong. This unknown man with the squeaking shoes who appeared after Mr. Piper had gone to bring the police . . . what can you tell me about him?"

"Nothing more," responded Waite. "He just came and went."

"That's every scrap we know about him, except that he had a high voice," added Harrison.

"Old or young?"

"Oh, definitely middle-aged, I think."

"And he didn't knock at the door?"

"No. There wasn't anything of that kind. He just oiled in with a latchkey, and we dashed out to nab him but fell over our own feet. By the time we'd picked ourselves up he had gone."

"That seems strange conduct. If he meant to come in, and had a latchkey, one would think that he . . ."

"Yes, it's a point," said Harrison. "I mean, if he'd only come to ask after Aumbry's health, it does seem odd that he scuttled off like that as soon as he heard a sound. You'd think he'd investigate, what?"

"It would depend upon what he came for."

"Yes, I suppose it would. But why should he come at night if he was up to any good?"

"Well, why did *you* come at night? Yet you assumed that you were performing a creditable action!"

"Yes, it was the diptych, you see. We did rather want to get it back."

"Oh, no. You wanted some amusement. I don't think the diptych enters into this, but, all the same, it would be interesting if we could find it. Where do you think it is now?"

Even Harrison's opinion of her fell when she asked this question.

"Do you think Bradley of Angelus was *deceiving* us?" he demanded in a whisper of Waite. The cackle with which Bradley's aunt indicated that she had heard this question reestablished her in Harrison's regard.

"Since it seems fruitless to ask any more questions," she said, "I shall leave you to brood (I hope) upon your sins, and go and report to the Chief Constable that I find you sobered by your experiences and misguided rather than criminal."

"Well, did you get anything out of them?" the Chief Constable enquired. Mrs. Bradley reported their story of having given a lift to the respectable manservant.

"And the next thing to be done, I imagine," she concluded, "is to contact those two Negro servants at Professor Havers' lodgings in Wallchester. They may or may not know what employees the professor had at Merlin's Castle, but it can do no harm to enquire."

"Ekkers has been on to them already, of course, but, beyond scaring the girl, he doesn't think he accomplished anything. I don't really think she and the chap (intelligent type, apparently) know anything that would be of use to us, but, anyway, at present the girl is too frightened and the man probably too clever to talk. Beyond swearing that the professor had no enemies (a statement which, from what we know of his record, is scarcely likely to be true) she merely babbled wildly of her innocence. Still, you may be able to work an oracle there. She's far more likely to talk to you than to a policeman. What did you make of our three young sprigs?"

"I think Mr. Waite could bear watching."

"Yes. I don't like the idea of a man turned thirty ragging about with those two young lads. There's something fishy there. Besides, he's a man of character."

"Of very determined character. He seemed to me a tough and ruthless man."

"Ruthless enough to commit murder?"

"I don't know yet, but I feel perfectly certain that something more than just ragging or any other kind of foolishness was involved. I suppose the diptych hasn't been found?"

"I'm doubtful whether it exists."

"I see. The one of the trio whom I am prepared to acquit of having had evil intentions is Mr. Harrison."

"What about Piper?"

"He strikes me as the playboy of the triumvirate. You noticed one odd thing about their story, did you? . . . That Mr. Waite, obviously the moving spirit in the affair, remained in the street and sent the other two to interview the professor?"

"Thought he'd be recognized, he says, and that the professor would not then trust them to go in search of the diptych. Says he used to bait the professor in lectures, and (in his own words) forfeited Havers' regard by so doing."

"That might be the explanation, of course. It is certain that he did not intend to risk being recognized, but whether the story of the baiting is true . . ?"

"Yes, quite, I see what you mean. There might have been deeper and darker reasons. Yes. I wouldn't put much past our Mr. Waite."

"Well, I'll go straight away to Wallchester and see those Negroes and also the professor's landlady. She may have something useful to report that she hasn't yet seen fit to tell the police."

The landlady, interviewed before Mrs. Bradley tackled the servants, proved tearful and tedious.

"Such a lovely gentleman, and so clever," was her burden. "Indeed, you could not have wished for a more considerate client. Always the rent up to date, and no late nights, and only the smallest parties."

"Ah, those parties," said Mrs. Bradley, who was considerably occupied by thoughts of the doll. "How often did he give them, would you say?"

The landlady was vague. With such a considerate, regular gentleman one did not particularly keep count. It might be one a month, not more. The moon? She could not say. She did not see what the moon could have to do with it, except that at full moon it might be easier for the guests to make their way home. Mr. Aumbry? Yes, she had heard that name mentioned, but she never went to the door herself. What were maids for? Mrs. Bradley, not too sweetly, asked to be allowed to interview the woman's maid, but the girl was as unhelpful as her mistress. She had heard the name of Aumbry, she asserted, but it was no business of hers who came to the house.

Mrs. Bradley, undefeated, undeterred, and (in the maid's view) extremely frightening, pursued the subject relentlessly. When had the last party been held? How many guests had attended it? Was Mr. Aumbry one of them? The maid cracked suddenly. Bursting into tears, she said:

"What's it all got to do with me? I never made him no doll's clothes!"

"Ah, yes. I wondered who had dressed the doll," said Mrs. Bradley with truth. "Who did? . . . because Professor Havers did not dress that doll himself."

"You better ask Bluna," sobbed the maid.

"His African servant?"

"Yes, her. Give me the creeps, she did, soon as I ever set eyes on her."

"You are prejudiced. Did Bluna have a sweetheart?"

"Yes, she did, too and all. Lives out on the Lansley Road. But I don't know why he ever come here. I don't know nothing about it. The professor engaged 'em both. It wasn't nothing to do with me."

Perceiving that even supposing she did know something more, this was not the time to seek further information, Mrs. Bradley again sought out the landlady.

"What has happened to Professor Havers' servant Bluna?" she enquired. "Are she and the colored manservant still here?"

"They both left here on Saturday, and I haven't set eyes on them since. Are you in with the police?"

"Yes, of course. Professor Havers has been murdered, and we want every detail we can get in order that we may track down his murderer. And, as Bluna's sweetheart did not live here, I fail to see how both could have left on Saturday."

"As to that," said the landlady, "this has always been a most respectable house."

"You've never had undergraduates for your lodgers, as I happen to know."

"How do you know that, pray?"

"Because you don't carry the *cachet* of the university authorities."

The woman looked daggers at her.

" 'Tisn't everybody wants that wild sort," she retorted at once.

"It isn't everybody who would have wanted Professor Havers," stated Mrs. Bradley mildly. "But more of that anon. I shall be obliged to you for Bluna's address."

"But I don't know it!" cried the woman. "I don't know where she's gone, and I don't care, neither. Her and that grinning sweetheart of hers! I'm thankful to be shut of the pair of them, and I hope I never set eyes on either one of them again!"

Mrs. Bradley, who had obtained part of the address of Bluna's fiancé from the maidservant, sought out the road and had no difficulty in obtaining the number of the house in which the mulatto was lodging. He came to the door himself, a teacloth in his honey-colored hand, and a woman's voice from the kitchen called:

"Who is it, dearie? Anybody for me?"

"No, I don't think so, Mrs. Richards," he answered. "I think it is about the late Professor Havers."

"Now how did you know that?" Mrs. Bradley enquired.

"I have followed your works for some time," he civilly replied, "and one of them in the Penguin edition has a photograph on the back cover. I know you investigate cases of murder for the baffled police force. That is right?" His broad smile was childlike and triumphant. "Please to come in. I have had the police here. I could tell them very little. I will tell you exactly the same."

"I hope not," Mrs. Bradley responded, stepping over the threshold. "I hope you'll be able to tell me all sorts of things which the police, perhaps, did not enquire about."

"That is an enticing thought. Please to come up to my room. It is bed-sitting, not only bed, otherwise it would not be nice to invite you."

"Dearie," called his landlady from the kitchen, "bring me back my teacloth if you're going to stand talking in the hall."

"Certainly, Mrs. Richards. Excuse me, please. I am drying the dishes, but police business must have first priority."

With another broad smile he vanished, and Mrs. Bradley could hear him in earnest conversation with his landlady. He reappeared shortly, still beaming, and invited her into the landlady's sitting room, a respectable mausoleum of family portraits and black, leather-covered horsehair furniture. Mrs. Bradley took one of the slippery armchairs and produced a notebook.

"Now, then, Mr. . . . . ?" she observed.

"Majestic. Mr. S. Majestic. My father's ship, I believe, or perhaps a hint as to conduct. I do not know. This room has been placed at our disposal by Mrs. Richards."

"That is extremely kind of her. Now, Mr. Majestic, you must forgive me if I seem to be intruding upon your private affairs. I understand that you are engaged to be married to Bluna, the late Professor Havers' servant."

"Yes, indeed. I also was employed by Mr. Havers."

"Is there a child on the way?"

The servant looked surprised but in no way offended.

"No. Oh, no. Nothing like that. I can wait until I am married," he said with dignity.

"I wasn't thinking of you," said Mrs. Bradley.

"You mean the professor? Oh, no, that is not his layout. The professor was not interested in girls except religiously."

"Religiously?"

"You understand, I am sure, that religion can be good religion or bad religion. Christian, Mohammedan, Buddhist, Jew, even Parsee and Hindu and Red Indian . . . those are good religion. Voodoo, all devil-worship, cannibalism, Artemis in Orthia, Diana of the Ephesians, all orgiastic rites . . . those are bad religion, but, still, religion."

"And Professor Havers was interested in bad religion?"

"Yes."

"But . . . forgive me . . . Bluna did not help him?"

"How should I know?"

"But you're prepared to marry her?"

"Oh, yes. She will make a good wife, and I want my son to be a Doctor of Divinity. If not Divinity, then of Laws. If not of Laws, then of Literature. But I will have him to be a Doctor, anyway."

"A child can inherit his mother's as well as his father's characteristics."

"Bluna has a good brain. Uneducated but good."

"And her morals?"

"She has none. She is a *good* girl."

"Did you ever see the Isaurian diptych?"

The complete change of subject did not take him aback. He smiled and spread out his large and beautiful hands.

"Often. I was very much surprised when Professor Havers gave it to Mr. Aumbry."

"*Gave* it to him?"

"Oh, yes."

"Under what circumstances?"

"There, I can scarcely tell. I was only Professor Havers' servant, you understand, but a valet hears a good deal. There was a compact between them. My diptych for your cooperation. So says Professor Havers in my hearing."

"Cooperation in what?"

"In magical rites."

"And did they cooperate?"

The servant spread his hands again.

"I do not know. Once the professor was changed for dinner I was free. I come back here to my good and dear Mrs. Richards, and get my supper and help to wash up. Then to my bed-sitter, as one says, and to study those books which I have been able to borrow from the professor's store."

"But what makes you think that Professor Havers *gave* the diptych to Mr. Aumbry?"

"I heard them discussing it. Mr. Aumbry had arrived at six o'clock, and before I took Professor Havers up to bathe and to dress him, there were drinks to be brought in, and, of course, the parcel."

"Ordinary, normal drinks?"

"Oh, yes. A very nice sherry and a sidecar I mixed myself."

"No cock's blood, or anything of that sort?"

"Oh, no!" He laughed joyously. "Nothing like that!"

"I suppose the magic doll was in the parcel. Had the professor ever used dolls before?"

"Yes, but brought by him into the house from a destination unknown to me. But once he had a cat image, not a doll. There was a suicide after that, Mrs. Bradley . . . Mrs. Lestrange Bradley, I should say."

Mrs. Bradley left the puzzling man and returned to Moundbury, where she saw the Chief Constable again.

"*Mio capitan*," she observed, "*nada tenéis que temer por vuestra tetera.*"

"How much?" the Chief Constable enquired.

"I merely suggest that you do not worry about your teapot."

"Why should I? Don't care much about tea, anyway."

"Oh, don't you know the story? It's a good one. A Spanish sailor was cleaning a beautiful solid silver teapot belonging to the captain of his ship when, unfortunately, he dropped it overboard. He went to the captain, and said, 'Captain, can a thing be said to be lost when one knows all the time where it is?' The captain replied that of course such a thing could not be lost. 'Then' said the sailor, 'have no fear for your teapot, for I happen to know that it rests on the bottom of the sea.' "

She smiled encouragingly. The Chief Constable did not seem to find the story amusing.

"I suppose you mean . . ." he began. Mrs. Bradley waved an attenuated yellow claw.

"I don't mean anything," she declared, "except that time, which, in due course, is bound to produce the teapot, is also, at present, on our side. What do you make of the maids who disappeared from Merlin's Castle?"

"Oh," said the Chief Constable, his face clearing, "we've traced the maids all right. That is to say, there weren't any. Needless to say, we're trailing that manservant the boys met and are going to hold him for questioning. But, as it happens, we've also hit upon a first-class suspect for the murder of Aumbry."

"Any connection with the murder of Professor Havers, I wonder?"

"Unfortunately, no."

"Yet the cases, I feel, must be connected."

"Yes, dash it, so do I. *Could* it have been those three boys?"

Mrs. Bradley shook her head.

"I really don't know," she replied. "And yet they're mixed up in the business. Somebody who knew that they were coming this way to try to regain the diptych took advantage of the situation, and murder resulted, one feels."

"I know. I think the same. But, as far as I can see, the only person who could possibly have known of their coming was Professor Havers himself, and he's one of the murdered men."

"Very difficult. Very difficult, indeed," said Mrs. Bradley; but her parchment countenance gleamed with unholy joy. "You were saying, however, that you had discovered another person who may have had some interest in the death of Mr. Aumbry."

"Yes." The Chief Constable proceeded to relate the strange story of Mr. Aumbry's will. "So we're going to ask Mr. Richmond Aumbry some questions," he concluded. "Harder questions than we asked him yesterday, I mean."

Mrs. Bradley wagged her head sorrowfully.

"Poor young man," she observed. "I wonder whether I might see him?"

"Yes, of course you can. But it does seem rather a coincidence that if Aumbry had lived a little longer he would most probably have remade his will in favor of the nephew whom he had always trusted and liked, Mr. Godfrey Aumbry."

"You mean Mr. Godfrey Ablewhite," said Mrs. Bradley, in a tone of reminiscence. The Chief Constable took no notice. He was not an addict of Wilkie Collins, and did not follow her train of thought. "Where does Mr. Richmond Aumbry live?" Mrs. Bradley added.

It proved that Richmond Aumbry lived in Wallchester. This might be coincidence only, Mrs. Bradley thought. She put it to the Chief Constable.

"Well, I don't know," he said. "It does seem a bit queer that Havers lodged there, too. Still, there seems no connection between Havers and Richmond Aumbry, and none between Richmond and the university."

"Richmond is a poet, you say?"

"He is alleged to be."

"You have not read his work?"

"Modern poetry is not in my line, you know."

"I didn't know. But it is very much in mine, and I feel that in Richmond's poetry lies the answer to our smallest and least important riddle."

"Which one is that? Oh, you mean whether or not he killed his uncle in order to inherit?"

"I would like to visit him," said Mrs. Bradley, without attempting to answer the questions. "Meanwhile, what happens to my clients?"

"Your what?"

"My clients. The Three Wise Men. The three gentlemen in the burning fiery furnace. The three men of Gotham who went to sea in a bowl. The three Norns. The Furies. The crown of triple Hecate. The three hostages of fortune. The Three Musketeers. The three clever monkeys. The three tiers of the royal crown of Egypt. The Three Blind Mice . . . that more than anything else . . . two of them, at any rate!"

"There are two things you haven't mentioned," said the Chief Constable.

"Both might be blasphemous, and blasphemy is the epitome of bad manners. So now for Mr. Richmond Aumbry's address. For 'carry the dead corse to the clay, and I'll come back and comfort thee.' "

"Comfort well your seven sons," retorted the Chief Constable. Mrs. Bradley, who had but two, hooted in admiration of this most apposite suggestion and took down the address which the Chief Constable hurriedly dictated. "And now," he added, "kindly suggest to Richmond Aumbry that the law is not really an ass."

"Take things as you find them," Mrs. Bradley replied. "Law, like pie-crust, was probably made to be broken."

"It happens, anyway," the Chief Constable disconsolately confessed. "Look at these wretched boys! Whether they were actually concerned in the murders or not, the fact remains that they were *there* . . . there in both houses, mark you! I'm guilty of *suppressio veri* and that's not at all a nice idea to go to bed with."

"You should try a wife," suggested Mrs. Bradley.

CHAPTER EIGHT

Merlin's Vivien

"She will fling dragons' teeth broadcast for you . . . and sweep away the prodigious crop,
and fling more, and show you that, though now a mumbling old crone,
she has had a tremendous past."

NOEL POCOCK—*An Adriatic Cruise*

The tall house to which Mrs. Bradley's chauffeur drove her was on the Milden Road and had obviously come down in the world. The door was opened by a colored girl who made the sign against the evil eye the moment she encountered Merlin's aunt.

"Ah," said Mrs. Bradley, "do you live here?"

The girl stood motionless in fright. Mrs. Bradley walked in and demanded to be taken to Mr. Richmond Aumbry. The girl fled, and Mrs. Bradley was left to contemplate either a hideous bead curtain which screened the kitchen regions from front-door visitors, or, if she preferred it, a sage-green wallpaper about a quarter of which had been torn off by (presumably) childish fingers, since childish scribblings were all over the rest of it to a height of three and a half feet from the floor. The linoleum was in holes, showing unwashed floorboards, and the only decorations, apart from some youthful attempts at art on the bare-plaster patches of the walls, were a couple of pictures hanging from nails. These depicted a sheep struggling in deep snow against a lurid winter sunset, and a dead fish lying across a basket of pears flanked by a jar of hollyhocks.

A door on the floor above opened, and a man's voice demanded angrily:

"Is that you, Phyllis? Or is it Bluna?"

"It is neither," Mrs. Bradley replied in her deep and lovely voice. "It is Fear, my little Hunter, it is Fear!"

"Then come on up," said the man disgustedly, "and don't waste my time if you can help it."

Mrs. Bradley responded to this invitation by climbing uncarpeted stairs to where a thin, unkempt, unshaven, extremely good-looking young man stood defensively upon the narrow landing.

"Good afternoon, Mr. Aumbry," she said. "I wonder whether you will be good enough to spare me a few minutes? I've come from the Chief Constable with reference to the murder of your uncle at Merlin's Furlong."

"That old Scrooge!" said Richmond. "Can't he lie still where he is?"

"I said his murder, Mr. Aumbry."

Richmond waved an agitated fountain pen so that a blob of ink flicked irritably on to the wall.

"What do you want?" he growled. "Here, perhaps you had better come in!"

"Thank you," said Mrs. Bradley.

In contrast to Richmond, the room into which he admitted her was remarkably neat and clean. He pulled forward an old but quite comfortable armchair, unearthed a packet containing three cigarettes, offered her one, smiled with relief when she refused it, lit one himself, screwed the top on his pen, and then, taking the cigarette from his mouth, said cheerfully:

"Well, they haven't arrested me yet."

"No," said Mrs. Bradley, "but unless we can obtain some very definite evidence of your innocence, that is only a question of time."

"But I didn't do it, you know." He smiled. "Uncle was a nuisance, particularly over that last will. In fact, I'm not at all sure that he hasn't avenged himself. There's no hatred like the hatred of love turned sour."

"He did once love you, then?"

"Oh, yes. Until I crossed him for good and all. And, mind you, I quite enjoyed scrapping with him. That's the devil of it now."

"The only devil is remorse," said Mrs. Bradley.

"Granted. Not that I feel overwhelmingly remorseful. But, look here, what do you want?"

"First, I want to know why Bluna, the late Professor Havers' woman-servant, is living in this house."

"How should I know? You'd better ask Phyllis. We can't really afford servants, but the poor girl can't cope with a job *and* the kids *and* the house."

"Who worked here before Bluna came?"

"Eh? Oh, a charwoman of sorts. An awful creature . . . dirty, slack, unreliable and a sneaker of rationed goods. You know the type."

"I have heard of it. It usually works for dirty, slack, unreliable and slightly unprincipled employers."

Richmond Aumbry laughed.

"*Touché*," he said, "but you mustn't blame anyone but me. Why on earth Phyllis sticks to me I don't know. And now this wretched business of my unlamented, screw-loose, abominable uncle! What did you say you wanted?"

"I am sent to find out what light you can throw on your uncle's death."

"None. I'm as much in the dark as everybody else. We all went there, as you probably know. By the way, you're not from the press, are you?"

"No. I have no connection whatever with the press. I am a friend of the

Chief Constable of South Moundshire and his fellow workers. By profession
I am a psychiatrist."

"Look here, I'm not mad, you know."

"No, no. I quite agree there."

"Oh, that's all right, then. I mean, if I'm arrested I'm quite fit to plead.
What are my chances, do you think?"

"Fifty-fifty," Mrs. Bradley callously replied. "Certainly not better than
that."

"I know." He looked gloomy and flicked ash on to the floor. Then he took
out his handkerchief and scrubbed the ash away again, finishing by rubbing
the sole of his shoe over the spot where the ash had fallen. "I suppose Uncle
Aumbry's will can stand?" he added. "If I'm not hanged for murder, I mean."

"Did anyone, apart from yourself, have any motive for killing your uncle,
do you know?"

"For killing him? No. He was a curmudgeonly old devil with a sense of
humor (*i.e.,* cruelty) all his own, but except for me . . . this wretched inheritance, you know . . . I don't think anyone had sufficient motive for killing
him. In fact, the thing's a mystery. I suppose it couldn't tie up in any way
with old Godfrey being hit over the head and his papers rifled, could it?
Because that was a queer do, too."

"I should like some details. When did this happen, and why?"

"*When*, I can tell you. *Why*, is completely beyond me. Uncle had invited
us all down, as he sometimes did, and got Godfrey to make out his will.
According to Godfrey (who's got no reason for lying) this will was what
everyone had expected. Godfrey was to get most of the boodle, Frederick
not much, and my brother Lewis and I were to get damn all. Then it appears
that Uncle Aumbry went out of the room to fetch something or other, and
while he was gone somebody sneaked in behind Godfrey, who had his back
to the door, clouted him over the head with some unspecified implement and
went off with his briefcase, rough draft and notes. Upon this, Uncle Aumbry
conceived the freakish notion of making a new will leaving everything to
me, which said document the old fool gave me to post to his London bank. It
was all according to Cocker, properly signed and witnessed, and somebody
was even sent out with me to make sure it went into the pillar-box. So you
see what a spot I'm in! The old devil most certainly intended only to lead me
up the garden, but before he could revoke the will and have it made out again
in Godfrey's favor (because without a doubt that's what he intended all along)
somebody bumped him off, and the police, quite naturally, have decided that
the somebody was me."

"Your alibi?"

"I haven't got one."

"None at all?"

"No. You see, at the time this seems to have happened I was dodging a bloke with a writ, so it didn't pay me to appear in public. I'd taken a job looking after a public lavatory in Keymouth."

"Why Keymouth?"

"Because I thought it wasn't a place my creditors were likely to think of. I literally went to earth, and it wasn't until I saw the report of Uncle Aumbry's death in an evening paper one of the clients gave me that I knew anything about it."

"But surely the local council. . . ?"

"Not a hope. It was a put-up job between the regular chap and me."

"But how did you hear of the job?"

"In the place itself. I'd thought of Keymouth because it's biggish and a good long way from Wallchester. I dived down into this place because I thought I'd spotted a chap who knew me, and the man in charge was bemoaning the fact that his stand-in was down with flu and so couldn't take his turn on duty, and I just chipped in and offered to do the job and we had it all fixed up in no time. He showed me the routine and I told him I'd do full time if he liked, as I was on the run from a woman who was trying to get me to the altar. It worked all right."

"Yes, but can't he supply you with an alibi?"

"Only one of sorts. There would be nothing to prove that I hadn't slid out, killed Uncle Aumbry and slid back again, you see. It isn't all that far from Merlin's Furlong to Keymouth. In fact, my other good reason for choosing Keymouth was that it wasn't a big fare from Merlin's Furlong where I was staying, of course. I had a note from Phyllis to tip me off that I was being served on, so I hopped it, and two days later Uncle Aumbry was killed."

"Hm!" said Mrs. Bradley. "And with his fortune you could have settled all your debts and freed yourself and your wife from a great deal of anxiety and discomfort!"

"Exactly. So you see what a spot I'm in."

"The police, of course, know that you were staying so close at hand?"

"Oh, yes. I've told them everything. It seemed the only thing to do."

"Would that all innocent but suspected persons were as clear-thinking and courageous!"

"You do think I'm innocent, then?"

"Such is my supposition at the moment. Now, tell me, Mr. Aumbry . . . even allowing for the fact that your uncle was a cruel old man . . . did not the new will which you posted occasion you a great deal of surprise?"

"Yes, in a way. Of course I didn't know the exact terms of the will. However, I knew my uncle. Under no circumstances whatsoever would he have permitted me to obtain any benefit from his money. I had accustomed myself to that idea. But he did indicate he'd made me his heir, and the fact that I knew it . . . and the others knew I knew it . . . doesn't really give me a fighting chance. It was so obviously I who killed Uncle Aumbry! You can't get away from that point. Nobody can. I myself can see it very clearly. Who stood to gain by Uncle Aumbry's death? I did. Far from being cut out of his will, I became the main inheritor of his property. Why shouldn't I have knocked him on the head before he had time to remake his will in favor of my cousin Godfrey, leaving me out of it all?"

"Why not, indeed?" Mrs. Bradley warmly concurred. "The only trouble is that it isn't in character."

"What isn't?"

"That you, my child, should ever do anything so crude, especially to gain an inheritance."

"Oh?" He seemed suddenly deflated. Mrs. Bradley kept a curious eye, meditative and medical, upon him. "I'd have you know that if I'd thought of this way of killing Uncle Aumbry without anybody having a clue to the murderer, I'd have killed him out of hand," he said defiantly.

"I don't believe it for an instant," said Mrs. Bradley. "But if you'd been the murderer there would have been clues in plenty. So far, there seems to be none except motive."

"But that sticks out like Boston Stump and one can't avoid spotting it. But, you know, if I committed murder and didn't intend to leave clues, I shouldn't leave any. I've plenty of brains." He looked at Mrs. Bradley in challenge, but she ignored the gambit, so, after a slight pause, Richmond added, "If only there were a hint of anyone else! But there isn't the smallest doubt that I'm the one and only suspect."

"You might be, if Professor Havers had not also been murdered. As it is, you have as good a chance of going free as anyone else. It is not you I am worried about; it is those three ridiculous, house-breaking undergraduates."

"Oh, they're all right. I know the type. They couldn't possibly have done in Uncle Aumbry."

"Did you, at any time, see the diptych, Mr. Aumbry?"

"What diptych?" He looked interested.

"The Isaurian diptych. The thing all the fuss was about in the first place."

Richmond smiled. "You may be surprised," he said cheerfully, "but really . . . do believe me! I don't know what you're talking about. Did the diptych belong to Uncle Aumbry? And has it been stolen? If so, you had better ask Godfrey about it. He was the only one in whom uncle confided at all."

"That can wait, then. And you really know of no enemy who might have hated your uncle sufficiently to kill him?"

"No one. Well, of course, there was this old Professor Havers. They were always at daggers drawn according to Godfrey. But as Havers himself has been murdered that certainly washes that out. They can hardly have killed each other like the Kilkenny cats, particularly as the bodies were some miles apart."

"Not so many miles. And according to Godfrey? Was he, then, in the habit of confiding your uncle's remarks to the rest of you?"

"No, only to Lewis. He and Godfrey are the respectable members of the family. Frederick lives on his wits and I live on my wife, but Lewis is an architect and Godfrey a solicitor."

"But Lewis, your brother, sometimes retailed what Godfrey had told him?"

"Oh, yes. Lewis and I are very thick, and we know we can trust each other. He's only five years older than I am, and we've always had lots in common."

"Gratifying. Now, Mr. Aumbry, I wonder whether I might see your wife for a few minutes . . . preferably not in your presence?"

"I'll see whether she's come in. She should be in about now." He went to the door and yelled downstairs. A girl's fresh, pleasant voice made immediate answer.

"Coming, darling!"

Phyllis Aumbry was about twenty-six, Mrs. Bradley guessed; a gray-eyed, graceful creature with a golden skin and a wide and friendly smile.

"My wife," said Richmond. "Mrs. Bradley, darling. She's going to keep my neck from the noose, we hope."

"Of course she is," said the girl. "I hope you haven't been giving too much away."

"It's your turn, anyway. She wants to ask you something about Bluna." He nodded to Mrs. Bradley and walked out, saying casually over his shoulder, "Fish and chips, or shall I open a tin?"

"Tin, I think, darling. The weather doesn't seem in tune with fish and chips."

"Right. Tea, coffee or beer?"

"Can we . . . ?"

"Yes. I got an advance on the estate from old Villiers. I pointed out that I haven't been hanged yet, and he coughed up fifty pounds."

"Fifty pounds? We could have a bottle of sherry!"

"Good idea. In fact, such a good idea that I got one. Also a bottle of port."

The girl's smile faded as soon as he had gone.

"Will it *really* be all right?" she asked hopelessly. "It seems watertight to us. Of course, he *didn't* do it, but innocent people have been convicted before this and . . . well, I expect he's told you! . . . we were really in a terrible spot for money. The poor boy published a book of poems at his own expense without telling me, and, of course, we haven't sold enough even to pay for the printing. The people were getting really nasty . . . not that I blame them . . . but I've persuaded Villiers, who isn't at all a bad sort, although he was

Uncle Aumbry's lawyer . . . to pay them off out of the estate. But it all looks so frightfully bad."

"It might do but for two factors," said Mrs. Bradley, "and to them we must pin our faith. First, Professor Havers has also been murdered, and, secondly, the Isaurian diptych seems to have disappeared."

"The Isaurian diptych? What on earth is that?"

Mrs. Bradley explained.

"And those boys tried to steal it back from Uncle Aumbry? What a joke, if it hadn't been for the murders!"

"Possibly. It has made things rather awkward for the boys."

"You mean. . . . Oh, but *they* wouldn't have killed Uncle Aumbry! And they certainly wouldn't have murdered Professor Havers!"

"Nevertheless, they broke into the two houses, an unfortunate coincidence for them."

"Yes. Queer, too. It's almost like Greek tragedy . . . inevitable, and nobody's fault, and all that. Don't you think so?"

Mrs. Bradley cautiously assented. Then she said, "What I really wanted to know was how the Negro girl Bluna comes to be in this house."

"Bluna? What has she to do with it?"

"I will tell you later, if you really don't know."

"Oh? Well, she came here to ask for a job, and I was so sick of our awful old Mrs. Pile that I took her on."

"References?"

"She didn't bring any, but there's nothing to steal here!"

"When did she come?"

"Only last week."

"What reason did she give for wanting work?"

"She didn't give any. She just asked me whether I wanted a maid, and said she could cook."

"And can she?"

"I don't know. I always get my lunch out. It's cheaper. We've got an office canteen. Richmond fends for himself and the children have school dinners, so we don't bother much with cooking, and, anyway, we can't afford much to cook with."

"You didn't know, then, that Bluna, up to the time of his death, was maid to Professor Havers?"

"Good heavens, no! How could I? I've never been to Professor Havers' house in my life. I say! That means the police sent her to spy upon Richmond! What a filthy idea!"

"So filthy that I don't think we need to connect it with the police. It raises some interesting points, though. May I speak to Bluna?"

"Yes, I suppose so." She called over the banisters, and, when the black girl appeared, was going out of the room when Mrs. Bradley called her back.

"I would like you to stay," she said. "You had better hear what I say to Bluna, and I would like you to take down her replies. You can write short-hand, I presume?"

"Yes. It's nice of you. Everything seems such a muddle, I'd be terribly keen to get even a bit of a line on something or other."

"I doubt whether Bluna will give us much help at present, but the coinci-dences in this case are quite alarming. Something is bound to come of them."

Bluna came in, wiping her hands very nervously down her apron, and stood just inside the doorway, obviously terrified but with a wide smile upon her handsome, innocent face.

"Ah, Bluna," said Mrs. Bradley kindly. "I am glad to find that you have got another good post since you left Professor Havers."

"Yes, madam," said the young maid, uncertainly.

"How did you come to hear of it?"

The girl's face brightened. She fumbled in the bosom of the cotton frock she wore under the apron and produced a letter.

"This was my recommendation." Except for an unmistakable intonation her English was perfectly correct.

Mrs. Bradley took the letter and opened it. A five-pound note crackled sharply. The letter itself was typewritten and the signature, P. S. Havers, was typewritten also.

> *To Bluna: This is from my brother Professor Havers to give no-tice he will not be coming back to Wallchester. Call at (here fol-lowed Richmond Aumbry's address) any time after six to get a new job.*

Mrs. Bradley handed the letter back, without the five-pound note. She took out her notecase, put five one-pound Treasury notes into Bluna's hand and said kindly:

"There you are. You can manage much better with those."

Bluna looked at her reverently.

"Say thank you to Mrs. Bradley," prompted Phyllis Aumbry. Bluna dropped a curtsey and fled, clutching the handful of notes in one muscular fist and the typewritten letter in the other. Mrs. Bradley, who still held the envelope, took out a pocket magnifying glass, and scrutinized it carefully.

"Delivered by hand. Not been through the post," she remarked. "I see the hand of the imperturbable manservant in all this."

"What manservant? Do you mean Bluna's sweetheart? He calls on her every evening. I think they're engaged. He helps wash up the tea-things and did the drains on Saturday afternoon before they went out together. He seems a very nice youth."

Mrs. Bradley did not mean Bluna's sweetheart but did not trouble to say so, and the conversation was interrupted by the entrance of Richmond Aumbry with a bottle of sherry and rather a job lot of glasses.

"Sorry this is all we can muster," he said. "Get anything out of Bluna?"

"Yes," Mrs. Bradley replied. "Far, far more than I expected. Will one of you please relieve her of that letter? I think it must be placed with the police. And now, I am wondering what would have happened if you had *not* engaged her when she called."

"There wasn't much chance we wouldn't," said Richmond at once. "Our Mrs. Pile was the world's worst. Everybody knew we'd give a lot to have a resident maid who could give an eye to the kids as well as keep the place going. I can't be disturbed when I'm working, and Phyllis . . ." he gave his wife an affectionate glance ". . . has bought it, anyway, in marrying me. The only trouble about a resident maid was the money, but Bluna comes for the same as we gave Mrs. Pile and says she doesn't want much to eat because her boyfriend lushes her up, so everything's very okey-doke."

Mrs. Bradley did not agree, but did not say so.

"Where was your cousin's briefcase found?—or did it vanish?" she enquired. Richmond looked puzzled, but Phyllis replied for him:

"It turned up in Godfrey's own bedroom, didn't you say, Rickie?"

"Oh, the briefcase! Yes, of course. Sorry. I didn't quite follow. It turned up in Godfrey's bedroom with the rough draft of the earlier will and all his notes and things. Nothing at all was missing. If it hadn't been for the bash on the head we might have wondered—but the knock he got was no joke, so we had to believe him about the briefcase."

(2)

"It seems logical," said Mrs. Bradley next day to the Chief Constable, "now that I have interviewed the nephew who, on the face of it, seems the most obvious suspect, to question Mr. Richmond's brother and cousins. There *must* be something they can tell me."

"You go ahead," said the Chief Constable. "Anything to be able to clear those three young idiots before the Long Vacation comes to a close! Why on earth couldn't they have old us sooner about that manservant? Because they left it so late, the inspector and his chaps have drawn a blank, so far as running him down is concerned. He doesn't seem to have been noticed at the station of Merlin's Ell, and nobody saw him take a train. Of course, it's such a tiny station that there are only a man and a boy, and they can't be everywhere at once, and as, at that time of day, no train was due on either platform, the chances are that the manservant's suitcase merely contained a change of clothes. If so, the probabilities are that all he did was to walk into the general waiting room, change, and walk out of the station again without anybody being the wiser. It's been done often enough in the past, and it will be done again. All we've got from these boys is a general picture of a neatly dressed, quiet-mannered fellow wearing morning clothes and a bowler. Stick the same bloke into tweeds, we'll say, or a waterproof and a snap-brim hat, and where are you? It's hopeless!"

"I agree with you that this manservant may know something about the death of Professor Havers," said Mrs. Bradley, "and that somehow or other he must be found. I also agree that finding him is likely to be difficult. What about the women servants he mentioned to our three adventurers . . . the cook and the two maids?"

"There never were any such persons. We've been able to establish that much. Oh, there's not much doubt that he's the murderer. Must be a pretty cool customer, too, as he doesn't seem to have turned a hair when he ran into those three boys. After all, they can witness to the time at which he left the house and can describe his appearance. If my men run him to earth he can be identified all right, I should think. The trouble is, of course, that the boys, finding themselves in a nasty mess, may have agreed to tell this yarn about the manservant, and we may simply be pursuing a shadow."

"You wonder whether they invented the man?" Mrs. Bradley enquired. The Chief Constable looked worried.

"Personally, I don't. I believe them. But the inspector is hard to convince, and, of course, the case is his pigeon. He argues, quite justly, that if the man really exists the boys would have mentioned him at once, if only to try to show the time at which they first arrived at Merlin's Castle. It's a pretty good point, too, because Professor Havers was undoubtedly killed before (according to what they've now decided to tell us), this manservant left the house."

"You think that the search for the man may be half-hearted, do you?"

"Oh, no, not a bit of it! Ekkers is a most conscientious officer and is no more prepared to suspect the boys unjustly than you and I are. All the same, that Waite chap is older than the others, and has got his head screwed on tight."

"I'm glad to hear it. Will you drive me to Merlin's Furlong, or shall I go by myself?"

"As you like. But, if it makes no difference to you, perhaps I had better come along."

"Good. You will then be answerable for my *bona-fides,* and that will save explanations. My position at present is strictly unofficial and meddlesome and my presence on the scene is, I fear some interested persons would say, completely unnecessary."

"I wouldn't say that the last two remarks were necessary. You didn't decide to meddle; the boys called upon you for help. You are certainly not unnecessary, considering the amount of trouble you've already saved us by tactful handling of those three solicitors. The boys' families were all up in arms."

"Ah, yes. I understand that the disappointed nephew, Mr. Godfrey Aumbry, is also a solicitor. I should like to see him first. He may be able to throw more light on his uncle's death than did the fortunate and highly suspect Mr. Richmond, although there were one or two points . . ."

"Yes, that's one thing; Godfrey is the last person to be suspected of having murdered Aumbry. He has lost a large fortune through his uncle's death. He and Lewis, Richmond's brother, are at work on Aumbry's papers and so forth, supervised, of course, by our men. Godfrey applied for permission, and there seemed no reason why we should not grant it, particularly as he and his other cousins have returned to the house, Merlin's Furlong, and are staying there for the present, so that we've got them under observation. It's really rather convenient. I wish Richmond would go and stay there too. You'd think he'd want to help Godfrey out."

"Was it their own suggestion that they should return and stay there?"

"It was Godfrey's suggestion, and the others, whose addresses he gave us, were perfectly willing to cooperate, except for Richmond, whom you've already seen. Richmond refused to leave his wife and children by themselves, or to bring them to a house in which murder had been committed. But we've got a man tailing him all the time, so, from our point of view, it doesn't matter much where he goes, so long as he doesn't attempt to leave the country."

"You've made up your mind, then, I take it, that he murdered his uncle?"

"No, no, I wouldn't say that. But he's a very poor man, and the motive sticks out a mile, so, naturally, our people are interested in him. Even so, he can't be held accountable for the death of Havers . . . not, at any rate, from the point of view of motive. There's no doubt, either, that all the cousins had left Merlin's Furlong by the time Havers was killed, and although we shall test their alibis I can't believe that there was no connection between the deaths. It seems incredible that two murders can have taken place within a few miles of one another—four miles, in point of fact, if one cares to walk over the hill—if there is no connection between them. Besides, they were of similar type. Yet I'm bound to admit that, as far as we've gone, it doesn't seem at all likely that any one person of those we have under review would have killed both Aumbry and Havers."

"Well, that saves time and trouble, in a way," Mrs. Bradley pointed out. "We look for two murderers, the second of whom may have discovered and copied the method of the first."

"Yes, but. . . ."

"It's so much easier," she insisted. "Approach the murders as two separate problems. Ignore the fact that they happened within a few miles of one another. After all, if a man was knocked on the head in Maida Vale and another in Shepherds Bush, the Metropolitan police would not necessarily suppose that they were connected."

"That's not an argument," protested the Chief Constable. Mrs. Bradley wagged her head in solemn agreement.

"Nevertheless, you will find it much simpler to tackle the deaths of Mr. Aumbry and Professor Havers separately," she insisted. "All roads may lead to Rome, but there's not much sense in confusing the Appian Way with Stane Street! Besides, you ignore the salient fact of Bluna's new post."

"Oh, the Negro girl! What's she to do with it?"

"I should like to have confirmation of a theory."

"What theory, though?"

"That one of the late Mr. Aumbry's nephews wrote to advise her that Richmond might employ her. After all, which of them knew of her existence? It is an interesting point."

"Yes, and which nephew had five pounds to spare! I quite see that. It certainly doesn't sound like Richmond, does it?"

CHAPTER NINE

Merlin's Nephews

"Yet I must beg you to explain yourself."

JOHN GAY—*The Beggar's Opera*

More than interested, now that she had interviewed Richmond Aumbry and had seen his wife, Mrs. Bradley pursued her enquiries by going to Merlin's Furlong, accompanied by the Chief Constable. There appeared to be nothing in common between the rest of Mr. Aumbry's nephews (who seemed, in fact, thoroughly suspicious of one another) and yet there was no doubt that the statements made by Godfrey, Frederick and Lewis indicated a refusal to believe that Richmond had killed his Uncle Aumbry.

"Of course, one can see that from the point of view of a prosecuting counsel, Richmond had a motive," said the lawyer Godfrey, "but I assure you that he is incapable of murder. On the other hand . . ." he frowned thoughtfully . . . "somebody (who was in this house at the time when my uncle drafted this last, ridiculous and, one fears, fatal will), *somebody,* I repeat, knocked me on the head and ran off with my papers."

"Indeed!" said Mrs. Bradley, as though she had not heard of this incident. "When was this?"

"Oh, three weeks ago. My uncle had invited my cousins and me to come and pay him a short visit. To me he had added that he proposed to make a will and that I might as well earn a few guineas as his own lawyer. We talked over his affairs and he told me definitely that he proposed to make me the chief beneficiary. I suggested that, if such was his intention, it would be far better to let his own man draw up the provisions. I did not want to be accused of having exerted undue influence. That would have been most distasteful. We are a united family, as families go, but people are extraordinarily unpredictable as soon as money comes into the picture."

"Very true." Mrs. Bradley nodded dolefully. "I wonder whether you would mind giving me some further details about the time you were knocked on the head?"

"Certainly I will. The notes of my uncle's first will were all prepared, and my uncle, who seemed in high spirits, went out of the room to get something he treasured so that I might see it, and, I think, congratulate him upon possessing it. Scarcely had he gone, leaving me alone in the room, when somebody must have stolen in and I was knocked unconscious. When I came to . . . I was not, I am thankful to say, very seriously hurt . . . the notes of the will had disappeared. It was after this that my uncle informed me that he was going to make a will in favor of my cousin Richmond. This he actually did . . ."

"The will which you consider ridiculous? I think you used that word just now."

"I did. Advisedly. It was my uncle's own business, of course, but he did it to upset and financially embarrass poor Richmond."

"By making him his heir?"

"By pretending to. It was a cruel and unnatural thing to do, for, having informed Richmond of the provisions, and so (he hoped), committed him to extravagances which Richmond could not have afforded on his income, he proposed to disinherit him in my favor. He told me this himself."

"There were no witnesses to your conversation, I take it?"

"None, so far as I know. But my uncle was in some ways a perverted moral type, and one never knew what he was up to. It would have been quite in character for him to have had someone in hiding . . . one of the servants, for example . . . who could testify afterwards to what had been said. He trusted nobody."

"Had he found the world in general unreliable?"

"I really have no idea. None of us saw very much of him. He spent most of his time in Wallchester where he became acquainted with this unfortunate Professor Havers. Then, occasionally, we would receive a summons to visit him here at Merlin's Furlong."

"Did all of you come every time?"

"Unless he invited me by myself . . . you will understand that my profession has made me rather more tactful and discreet than the others, and therefore I got on with him better than they did . . . we all came, even Richmond, whom he actively disliked."

"But, in spite of this dislike, Richmond thought he might, in the end, gain something from these visits?"

"I scarcely think so." Godfrey smiled . . . a tight, catlike, mirthless grimace . . . and added, in a lighter tone, "He came to annoy Uncle Aumbry. The dislike, one might call it hatred, was entirely mutual. They used to indulge in verbal sparring matches, and Richmond would call uncle names. He used invariably a reflective, almost episcopal tone of delivery which used to drive uncle insane. Uncle would have back at Richmond with taunts about allowing his wife to go out to work, and of having to send his boys to a council school. Coming here was about the only kind of holiday Richmond ever had, and uncle would tell him that, too, and lash out on the subject of poets and poetry, and people who were too lazy or too incapable to take an honest job and support their dependents."

"Then Richmond is a poet?" asked Mrs. Bradley as though she had not heard of this before.

"So he says."

"Published?"

"Two slim volumes, I believe. I haven't read them."

"Have you any idea who the somebody was who hit you and took your papers?"

"It wouldn't be fair to say."

"You mean it was Frederick Aumbry?"

"You say that. I do not."

"Fair enough. I won't interrupt your work any longer. I wonder where I can find Mr. Lewis Aumbry?"

"I'll send for him."

"No, no. All your papers are here, and I don't intend to disturb you. I'll find him for myself."

"Well, he's bound to be about somewhere," said Godfrey, settling himself at his desk, "and if I can be of any further assistance, you know that you can call upon me." Upon second thoughts, he got up and opened the door for her. Mrs. Bradley ran into Lewis in the passage.

"Yes, I did listen," he said, before she could speak to him. "So would you if that caddish person in there was doing his best to put a rope round your brother's neck! Richmond didn't do it. He couldn't have done it. It isn't in him, and that's that."

"But that is exactly what your cousin Godfrey has just told me," Mrs. Bradley protested. Lewis snorted and did not reply. "I very much want to talk to you," she added, "and, since you have overheard the conversation between Mr. Godfrey and myself, perhaps you will be good enough to give me your own interpretation of the facts."

"Certainly. May I ask how you come into the affair?"

Mrs. Bradley, accompanying him to a grim small chamber whose mullioned window looked out on to the courtyard, seated herself and told, with satirical humor, the story of her three intrepid, misguided undergraduates.

"Young fools!" said Lewis. "And, because of them, my brother is landed in this ghastly mess!"

"An unfair observation!" Mrs. Bradley retorted. "Whoever killed your uncle, your brother, who had so much to gain by your uncle's death, was bound to come under suspicion."

"Do *you* suspect him?"

"I don't know enough facts yet to suspect anybody, but I have had a talk with your brother."

"Yes?"

"He is not, I would say . . . I am speaking now as a psychiatrist . . ."

"You're not . . . good heavens! Of course! You must be! Mrs. *Lestrange* Bradley, isn't it?"

"Yes."

"Then my brother," said Lewis, with complete conviction, "is safe. You'll have decided already that it isn't in Richmond's nature to kill anybody."

"I was about to say that he did not seem to me a criminal type. Murder, of course, is a different matter entirely. It is a sin, rather than a crime, and it is a point of view rather than either. I should hesitate to say that your brother would commit murder for gain, but I would not say that under no circumstances would he kill, and your uncle appears to have tried him very high."

"Yes, he did. Richmond has the best brains of the lot of us, and as a boy he was Uncle Aumbry's favorite. Uncle took it badly when Richmond declined to partner him in his business and took to literature. He took it very badly indeed."

"What *was* your uncle's business?"

"I think he was a receiver of stolen goods," said Lewis calmly. "But I've no proof, of course." Mrs. Bradley thought of the story told her by the three students and reserved judgment.

"This attack on Mr. Godfrey," she remarked. "Have you any theories?"

"None, except that neither Richmond nor I could have made it."

"That leaves Mr. Frederick, then."

"Richmond and I were together. He was telling me what he would do to Uncle Aumbry if there were no law against it."

"And what would he have done to Uncle Aumbry?"

"Killed him, of course," said Lewis, looking surprised.

"And you think that is proof that he did not kill him, I suppose."

"Well, what do *you* think? Besides, when could he have done it?"

"Surely that is what we have to find out?" She deserted Lewis and went in search of his cousin Frederick. Frederick was in his own room, a chamber in that tower which the three undergraduates, according to their own account, had not explored.

"Mr. Frederick Aumbry?" she asked, admitting herself without invitation. Frederick Aumbry was testy.

"I don't see what all the fuss is about," he growled. "Uncle Aumbry had been asking for it for years. Neither my cousins nor I killed him. I except Godfrey. A graceless ass, if you ask me, and much too sure of himself."

"I *am* asking you," Mrs. Bradley responded. "Do you *really* think your cousin Godfrey killed your uncle?"

"*Since* you ask me," Frederick replied ungraciously, "actually I don't. But what the hell is it to do with you?"

Mrs. Bradley patiently pointed out that she was vouched for by the Chief Constable.

"Well, I don't see it," said Frederick, without attempting to explain what he meant. Mrs. Bradley did not press him; she merely remarked:

"And who hit your cousin Godfrey and rendered him unconscious?"

"Whoever it was has my blessing," said Frederick, sweeping back his honey-colored hair.

"But you must surely have a theory," Mrs. Bradley persisted. "You yourself, for instance. What were you doing at the time?"

"No idea. Wait a minute, though! Yes, I have! I was writing a letter to the papers. I remember, because Uncle Aumbry put his head in at the door, made a rude noise, and went away again. I didn't finish the letter because I wanted a reference. I went down to the library, but the door must have been locked. At any rate, I twisted the handle, but nothing budged, so I came back in here, and the next thing was all this hullabaloo about Godfrey. Then came dinner, and a general row in which we were all involved except Godfrey, and then I went off to the village pub, as was my custom after one of uncle's dinners, and spent most of the evening there."

"I notice that your first statements are incapable of proof."

"I know. They're the truth, though." His attitude of belligerence was gone. "Look here, who *did* kill Uncle Aumbry? I wish I knew. It's abominable to suspect poor old Richmond!"

"I might hazard a guess," said Mrs. Bradley. "Was there any reason why the library door was ever locked?"

"Perhaps there was. Uncle kept his safe in there, built into the wall."

"What was kept in the safe? Money?"

"I've no idea. I never thought about it, and uncle certainly never confided in me."

"Mr. Aumbry, suppose it were put to you directly that your cousin Richmond killed your uncle in order to benefit from a will which he felt was bound to be altered if your uncle lived, what would you say?"

"Same as I've said all along. I don't understand Richmond much. I think he's an ass. Anybody who thinks he can live by writing poetry is an ass. Why don't he take up a profession like Godfrey and Lewis, or follow the winners, like me? There's sense in that. But poetry! Who wants poetry, anyway, except it's something for brats to learn at school? But to suspect him of murder, whatever his reason might be, is just plain out-and-out cuckoo!"

"One more question, Mr. Aumbry, if you will be so good. This last will that your uncle made: did *you* think he intended to let it stand?"

"Oh, no, certainly not! He was always trying to take a rise out of Richmond. Not that he got much change out of it! Richmond knew he had no expectations, so he used to say what he liked to uncle, and, having the gift of words, so to speak, could get under the old boy's skin and drive him nearly crazy. Why, Richmond himself knew perfectly well that the new will wouldn't stand."

"It must have been a great temptation, then, to make certain that it did," said Mrs. Bradley. Frederick's eyes protruded indignantly.

"Nothing of the sort!" he declared. "I've told you the truth because I'm not over-blessed with brains and it takes brains to be a good liar, but Richmond is absolutely out of it. Too few guts and too much imagination for a murderer. No question about it. If he told me himself he'd done it I shouldn't believe him."

"Can you throw any light on this strange business of your cousin Mr. Godfrey having been knocked on the head and his papers taken?"

"I've been thinking a lot about that," said Frederick slowly, "and I've come to the conclusion that it was either Uncle Aumbry's murderer or the old man himself. He was a queer old codger, you know. Not a single moral instinct except he was a monk about women. Never knew him to look at a skirt, except my late aunt. But in all other directions Fagin could have learnt a lot from him."

"And you think he may have been the person who hit Mr. Godfrey on the head?"

"More than likely. If he had a suspicion that Godfrey had put down a few things off the record he'd have had no scruples about getting to know what those few things were. Or he may have thought Godfrey would do a bit of private snooping while he was out of the room."

"Would that be in character?"

"In Godfrey's character, you mean? Oh, yes. If Godfrey thought there was anything worth finding out, it wouldn't stay hidden very long."

"Yet Mr. Godfrey was your uncle's favorite nephew, was he not?"

"I was never altogether sure," said Frederick thoughtfully. "They were birds of a feather, in a way, but I always thought that if Richmond had played his cards right he could have been the apple of the old man's eye. When we were boys there was no doubt about which of us Uncle Aumbry liked the best. But Richmond's poetry, and then his marriage, ditched his chances of the money. The old man was only ribbing him when he made that new will, as I've already made plain."

"What do you know about the Isaurian diptych, Mr. Aumbry?"

Frederick gaped at her.

"How did you get on to that?" he asked. Mrs. Bradley told him the story of the three undergraduates.

"Silly young fools," said Frederick. "Why, if Uncle Aumbry had been alive when they came here, they'd have had a twelve-bore loosed off at their heads!"

"You do not disapprove of the actual fact that they broke in, then, apart from the danger to themselves?"

"Certainly not. The old boy was a jackdaw, to put it mildly. Anything he saw that he fancied, well, his hooks were on it in no time."

"So you think he *did* steal the diptych from Professor Havers?"

"Think? I know he did! At least, that he'd stolen it from somebody. It definitely wasn't his own."

"How is that, Mr. Aumbry?"

"Well, I'd backed a few losers and I wondered whether Uncle Aumbry was good for a touch. No! I'll be truthful. I knew he wasn't, but I thought I might be able to sneak something I could pawn. The old man had such a vast collection of odds and ends that I felt pretty sure I could hook on to something which would see me through until I could recoup. Of course, I intended to get the whatever-it-was out of pawn when I was in a position to do so, and shoot it back where it belonged. Nothing wrong, you see. Just temporary accommodation."

"I see. And . . . ?"

"I descended upon uncle just before the Grand National . . . not that I ever bet on steeplechases . . . much too chancy. No, I stick to the flat, don't you?"

Mrs. Bradley, who never betted on horse races, agreed that it was a wise plan.

"So much easier to estimate form," she added, hoping that this comment would pass muster.

"Exactly," said Frederick. "Well, you've realized what sort of a place this is. Apart from a couple of Chinese houseboys and a Kanaka cook . . . all of whom seem to have made themselves scarce, incidentally, so we've had to get help from Merlin's Ell . . . there was nobody to study the comings and goings of visitors. I just breezed into the courtyard, gave the Chinks a couple of bob each and the Kanaka a pretty hot tip for the Oaks . . . sporting chap, that Kanaka, always a pal of mine, really . . . so that they got the idea to stay put and let me announce myself to uncle, and then I went up to the other tower where he kept the bulk of the loot."

"The three undergraduates did not find your uncle's collection," Mrs. Bradley pointed out.

"Simple. Trapdoor under the floor of the Queen's Bedroom. Covered by a strip of nailed-down carpet. Only—the nails are screws. Well, in I crept, but there was uncle, with the carpet up and the trapdoor open, so pleased with what he was handling that he didn't even hear me come in. I was wearing sneakers, of course, as a precaution against sound, but he was pretty well absorbed."

"The diptych, of course."

"The diptych. I greeted him breezily and he jumped a couple of furlongs and let out some pretty frenzied comments. I soothed him down, and, perceiving that a snatch was out of the question, I asked him for a temporary loan. He cursed me and told me where I could go, so I told him where he could go, too, if I described to the police the little treasure he was crooning over so tenderly. So, of course, we made a deal."

"And on this you base the assumption that the diptych was not, in fact, your uncle's property?"

"What would you have assumed?" asked Frederick with the broad smile of a man who has taken fortune at the flood. "I asked him for a hundred pounds, and I got it. Not a loan. A free gift, the old scoundrel. Unluckily, I lost the lot at Goodwood."

Mrs. Bradley left him to his mixed bag of memories and returned to his cousin Lewis, brother to the poet Richmond.

"I believe you are an architect," she said. Lewis, with his pleasant smile, admitted it.

"Council houses and flats, and county police stations, mostly," he added.

"You like your profession?"

Lewis looked surprised.

"Why else should I follow it?" he asked. "If I wanted to write poetry I should write it. I don't. I prefer to do my thinking in terms of stresses and strains, space, light, the fusion of materials and design."

"A poet in bricks and mortar," said Mrs. Bradley.

"In ferro-concrete and breeze," retorted Lewis.

"*Did* your brother kill your Uncle Aumbry?"

"I tell you he couldn't kill anything except a misplaced accent in sprung rhythm."

"When did you last see the Isaurian diptych?"

"The what diptych?"

"The Isaurian diptych. It was probably your uncle's most precious and valuable possession. He is thought to have stolen it from the late Professor Havers."

"That wouldn't surprise me, but I've never been shown any of Uncle's Aumbry's stuff since I was twelve. I said thought he was a receiver. I didn't know he'd ever turned his hand to the actual job of acquiring by stealing, but I'd never put it past him. He was a completely villainous old man."

"What did you make of his new will, the one in favor of your brother?"

"As a matter of fact, I'm not at all sure what I think. I wouldn't be surprised if the old man meant it to stand. He was such an old devil that I can quite imagine him double-crossing the obliging and obsequious Godfrey just for the fun of it, you know."

"Thank you very much, Mr. Aumbry," said Mrs. Bradley with real gratitude. "I'm not at all sure that yours is not the most helpful statement I've listened to yet, unless I except that proffered by your cousin Frederick."

"Frederick? He's a bit of a heel, you know."

"Yes, yes, the Achilles tendon is sometimes. . . ."

"At the root of all evil? Yes, I expect you're right. Frederick's Achilles tendon is money, and always has been."

"So much is clear to me, not least of all from Mr. Frederick himself. But I was about to observe that the Achilles tendon is sometimes the key to a man's conduct. You say that your cousin Frederick is a heel, but have you never heard of showing a *clean* pair of heels?"

Lewis looked at her doubtfully for a moment; then his face cleared and his gentle smile irradiated it.

"Good old Frederick," he said. "Somewhere, you mean that, ass as he is, he's cleared Rickie?"

"I wouldn't say that," said Mrs. Bradley, "but I would say that he shows an innocent, confiding nature."

"So do his bookies," said Lewis. "I can't see why the devil they still allow him credit. But what did he say to help my brother?"

"He confirmed my own suspicions, that is all, and does not know he did."

CHAPTER TEN

Merlin's Choice

". . . but yet I learned perfectly that it is no marvel at all though men in a wind lose their length in shooting, seeing so many ways the wind is so variable in blowing."

ROGER ASCHAM—Toxophilus

With such knowledge as she felt she had gained from her interviews with old Mr. Aumbry's nephews, Mrs. Bradley returned to the Chief Constable, whom she found in the courtyard.

"Yes, the inspector has traced the three servants," he said, when she had reported her conversations. "They're scared stiff, of course, but they've got watertight alibis for the time of the death. It seems that whenever any dubious transaction was on hand, the old man used to send them out on the spree so that he was alone in the house to finish his business. They've been positively identified as being elsewhere on the night of his death, because the Kanaka got so drunk that he was locked up, and the two Chinks were pinched in Southampton for peddling dope. We can absolutely wash them out. As for Havers, there's no evidence they'd ever heard of him."

"Where is the Kanaka now?"

"Still in quod. You see, he assaulted the policeman who was assisting him towards the police station. The magistrates took a grave view and handed him a month."

"These three men appear to have behaved with great commonsense, both from their point of view and our own."

"Well, yes, it does help," the Chief Constable admitted. "The odds, then, are still on Richmond Aumbry."

"No one but you seems to think so. Even Godfrey, who might be excused for feeling sore about the will, is positively certain that Richmond is incapable of murder. Besides, it seems to me that we've another suspect now."

"Oh? Who?"

"The unknown person on whose behalf the three servants were granted leave of absence."

"Yes, but we've no proof that such a person ever came to Merlin's Furlong that day. We made enquiries, naturally, as soon as we learned that the servants could produce these alibis, but nobody in the village noticed any stranger passing through, and strangers, especially strangers in cars, would be pretty obvious in Merlin's Ell, one would have thought."

"Suppose the stranger had come by night and was already in the house when the servants were sent out of it?"

"Suppose what you like; there's nothing to prove it."

"In other words . . ."

"In other words . . . stymie," said the Chief Constable.

"I'm not so sure," Mrs. Bradley replied. "The first question we have to answer, it seems to me, is why the lawyer Godfrey was hit on the head, and by whom, and I have told you what Frederick Aumbry told me about that. And Frederick struck me, on the whole, as, at least, an impartial witness."

"There's one thing," said the Chief Constable, "from all the evidence we have at present, it still seems that Godfrey Aumbry had every reason to desire to have his uncle alive. It seems certain that the old man intended to make him his heir."

"Against that, surely, is the extremely shrewd remark by Frederick that old Mr. Aumbry may, after all, have been the person who hit Mr. Godfrey on the head. Then, Lewis half-thinks the inheritance was for Richmond and Aumbry was playing cat and mouse with Godfrey. It is interesting, too, to note that none other of the nephews seems to have had *that* idea. They are certain that the will drafted in Richmond's favor would not be allowed to stand."

"Yet it does stand, which brings us back to Richmond. But you still don't believe that Richmond killed his uncle."

"No, I don't."

"Irrational, isn't it?"

"Entirely, from your point of view."

"Feminine intuition?"

"There is no such thing. Women are poor debaters (with notable exceptions, of course) and often find it impossible to make their reactions the subject of a logical argument; but, none the less, they have always 'something to go on,' as the saying is. Their perceptive powers are often livelier than those of men, who are apt to be ponderous and slowwitted on the question of human relations, and therefore women arrive at the truth with what is, to men, unfair leaps in the dark over logical fences and obstacles. I don't believe Richmond Aumbry is a murderer because, although he might kill in a fury, he would not kill for gain."

"How can you be sure of that, though?"

Mrs. Bradley grimaced.

"If he would kill for the sake of his wife and children he would have done it for their sakes before now, I should imagine," she said drily. "And that brings me to one of the logical fences over which I may have seemed to you to have leapt. Richmond is a poet. All his natural pugnacity and violence have gone into the forging of his poems. He might, as Shelley did, write of such horrors as the story of the Cenci, but it would never occur to him to translate those horrors into reality. His dislike of his uncle, his deep affection for his brother Lewis, his contempt for Frederick the saloon-bar man and for Godfrey the stick-in-the-mud, could all be sublimated, as could any bitterness he might feel at living on his wife's earnings and being unable to give his sons the education for which he feels they are probably fitted. No, no. Richmond Aumbry is not our man."

"Well, it couldn't be Godfrey, anyway."

"Are you sure of that? Personally I have an open mind, and I doubt very much whether it was Frederick, for Frederick is an uncouth, natural man, and if he had killed his uncle he would have blazed such a trail that by now you would have had him in custody."

"That leaves us Lewis. He is fond of his brother. Might have seen a chance of putting him on velvet, and decided to take it, you know."

"Why? He believes his brother to be a happy man."

"Yes, but Richmond would probably be a lot happier if he had his uncle's thousands at his back."

"There are no degrees in happiness," Mrs. Bradley pointed out. "Either one is happy or one is not."

"You don't think a happy man would be happier if he had a fortune?"

"If he would be happier with a fortune he could not have been happy without one."

"You don't think Lewis killed his uncle, then?"

"I think it extremely doubtful."

"Well, I'm going to have another look at Mr. Aumbry's will. Others slightly stood to benefit besides Richmond, and there may be one to whom even a small amount of money would have come in very useful. After all, a hundred pounds can save many an awkward situation. Suppose Frederick, for example, had been stuck with a gambling debt, or had backed someone's bill, or had had to buy off a woman . . ."

"What an imagination you have!" said Mrs. Bradley admiringly.

"Well, in those sort of circumstances, can you see Frederick Aumbry as a murderer?"

"With the naked eye."

"The first encouraging word you've spoken since this conversation began."

"We have no evidence that Frederick Aumbry had any of these difficulties. And there's another thing . . ."

"We'll soon find out whether he had. In fact, every one of these nephews, even Godfrey. . . ."

"The motiveless Godfrey. . . ."

". . . will have to explain exactly where he was and what he was doing at the time of his uncle's death."

"I thought they had all been questioned already by the police about that."

"Well, they have, but there's nothing like a certain amount of repetition for getting at the truth."

"So Torquemada believed," said Mrs. Bradley distastefully. "Besides, you won't get any more from those nephews."

"Why not?"

"Because Lewis and Richmond are speaking the truth, Frederick, in spite of what he says, has an excellent memory for what he said last time (whether it is the truth or not) and Godfrey, because of his training in law, will see through every question you ask him and will answer to his own advantage. But I was about to remark . . ."

"Well, we'll tackle the truth-tellers first," said the Chief Constable, "and find out whether truth isn't double-faced as well as double-edged. I'll send Ekkers over."

"But I was about to remark," repeated Mrs. Bradley firmly, "that Frederick had his own means of raising money from his uncle, and would not have killed the goose which had suddenly begun to lay golden eggs."

"Oh, the blackmail business he mentioned! Yes, of course, that's a point. We'd better explore that hidey-hole in the floor. I suppose the diptych is there."

(2)

"I've told you already," said Lewis Aumbry in resigned tones, "that on the day of my uncle's death I was playing golf at Sandwich. I've given you the names of my partner and of my opponents. You've questioned them and they bear out what I say. What more can I add? I didn't kill a seagull in flight, I didn't even get a birdie, and I didn't stay for a drink at the nineteenth. I went home and had a bath, then I dined at a restaurant in Greek Street where they know me and can swear to me, and then I went to my club and stayed until midnight. I could scarcely have returned to Merlin's and killed my uncle before three o'clock next morning. What else do you want to know?"

"Nothing, sir," the inspector morosely replied. "I'm off now to interview your cousin, Mr. Frederick."

"Much good may it do you! Anyway, good luck!"

"Account for my movements on the day and night of my uncle's death? Can't do that, old boy," said Frederick, shaking his head. "Honor of a gentleman involved, and all that sort of thing. However, this much I'll tell you. I was in my flat—you've got the address—from about eleven pip emma. Had been flung out of a pub in or near Leicester Square just before closing time. Can't remember which pub—too sozzled—but you'll be able to find it. I expect they all know me round there. Anyway, I managed to get home without being pinched, and after that—well, I expect you know the ballad of the dear little thingummy's daughter? What? And that's as far as I'm prepared to let the poor young baggage down. Anything else we can do for you?"

"Nothing, sir." He had the fatalistic feeling that Frederick's alibi would be foolproof. He went off to interview Richmond.

"Where was I?" asked Richmond incredulously. "Good heavens, I've already told you where I was! Why should I attempt to recall these revolting details? If you think I killed my uncle, well, pinch me for it and make yourself look damn' silly."

The inspector gave it up and called upon Godfrey. Godfrey was ready with chapter and verse.

"I have nothing different to say, but I can add a little," he promised. "On the night when, according to the medical evidence, my uncle died, I had been at a public dinner in London. It is a pity, apparently, that I was not one of the after-dinner speakers, but, all the same, I assure you that I did not leave my place at table until we broke up at about eleven. The dinner was held at the *Chamoisie* and after it I went back to my flat and played bridge for a couple of hours with three friends who have agreed that I should give you their names and addresses. If you think that I could have left my flat at about half-past one and driven down to Merlin's Furlong and killed my uncle after he was dead . . . !"

"No, no, sir, of course not. But you, in your profession, will realize I have to make these routine enquiries to fill in my report. I'd better have those names and addresses, though, so as to square everything up."

"I hope you will not only take the names and addresses, but that you will call upon the persons concerned," said Godfrey austerely, "and satisfy yourself that what I have said is correct."

"It's a job for the Yard now, sir," said the inspector, reporting to the Chief Constable. "Three out of the four of those nephews live in London."

"I don't think we'll trouble the Yard yet, you know, Ekkers. Richmond lives in Wallchester, and he's the obvious suspect still, from the point of view of motive. Besides, it might be said that he refuses to account for his movements. By the way, I suppose there's still no trace of that manservant those three boys mentioned?"

"In a manner of speaking, yes, sir."

"That sounds promising."

"It's about as promising as the four-and-twenty blackbirds in the pie, sir," the inspector lugubriously announced. "In other words, there just isn't any such person."

"The professor had no manservant, do you mean?"

"Exactly that, sir. When he left his lodgings in Wallchester to come down here, he used to manage with a couple of women from the village. There were no regular servants at Merlin's Castle, as we found out before, and the professor has never employed a gentleman's gentleman in his life, except the negro we've already interviewed, and he seldom came down to the Castle."

"That's rather interesting."

"It may be interesting, sir, but I must say it's depressing. We've wasted a lot of time."

"Not all that much. Cheer up, man. We now know two things about the fellow that we didn't know before. We know he wasn't a manservant, and we know he wasn't a local chap. Wallchester is your hunting ground again, I rather fancy."

"Our enquiries there are likely to end in smoke, sir. We've simply nothing to go on, except to pinch Mr. Richmond Aumbry."

"Look here, suppose we take these three young idiots and give them to you as your assistants? After all, they've seen this man at very close range, have talked to him, and ought to be able to spot him again even if he's entirely differently dressed. We've told them they must hold themselves at our disposal."

"Suppose he's acquired a beard, sir? If they could hear his voice I'd say there was a chance, but it's all too easy to change a clean-shaven chap's appearance."

"Yes, that's true. Oh, well, if you think it's no go, we'll leave it alone. Anyway, they might be more nuisance than they're worth. Perhaps we could lease them out to Mrs. Bradley! She's probably far better able to keep the tabs on them than we are. Where are they now?"

"Still lodging with the sergeant and me, sir. They're paying right well, I'll say that."

"Well, I'm glad we discharged them with a few solemn words. I'm certainly not prepared to jug them, even for breaking and entering. A blind eye had to be turned to the fact that they got into those two houses. I'm rather glad they did, as a matter of fact. As we've said before, it has brought us into these cases days before we might have found out anything, and that is certainly something to be thankful for, particularly in the case of Professor Havers, who'd been so recently killed."

"As you say, sir. As their fathers' lawyers have been at some pains to point out, there's such a thing as *Habeas Corpus*. We couldn't have held them without charging them with something, even if not with murder. We'd have been on the wrong side of the law altogether."

Harrison had been greatly impressed by the Chief Constable's magnanimity.

Piper (who had been carrying on a flirtation with the sergeant's daughter and was achieving his usual success in such matters) was slightly regretful to be given his freedom so soon, and Waite, by far the most single-minded and purposeful of the party, was quietly and ruthlessly preparing to turn their promised detective work into the rag of the season.

"You note," he observed, when they were in their car and Piper was driving eastwards and to the north, "there is nothing to stop us denouncing in turn every senior member of the university to the police as somebody we recognize to have been this smooth person we drove to the station."

"After the second or third attempt we should be sent down for good," objected Harrison.

"Not if we select our victims with sufficient care. I may even fly higher, and denounce the president of the Union or, better still, one of the female dons. The possibilities are endless."

"So endless that, so far as I am concerned, they're not even going to begin," said Harrison firmly. "Peter, we're being waggled at by somebody's chauffeur."

Piper pulled up beside a gesticulating man in uniform.

"I beg your pardon, sir," said the man, "but I believe you are the gentlemen who are on your way home from the murders."

"Aptly put. We are," replied Piper. "Who are you?"

"I am Mrs. Bradley's chauffeur, sir. My employer would be glad of a word with you if you could spare the time."

"Well, I expect it is largely due to her that we're not in jug," said Waite cordially. He got out of the car and the others followed. The chauffeur led them to a large limousine which was parked a dozen yards ahead.

Mrs. Bradley greeted them kindly, informed them that they were looking extremely well, and then came to the heart of the matter.

"Before the Long Vacation ends," she said, "we have to identify two murderers."

"I thought it was only one," said Waite.

"The police may have given you that impression, Mr. Waite, but I have reason to think that I am right. Nevertheless, I must have evidence, and there is nobody better able to help me to get it than one of you three."

"*One* of us? The inspector told us all three."

"One only. The point is to decide which one. I think I'll get out of the car and look you over."

"*Why* only one?" asked Piper, opening the door for her.

"Because the other two must occupy themselves with the work to which they should have been giving their close attention during the Long Vacation. Besides, I should be conspicuous if I took three of you about with me. Now, then: from previous conversations with you I have formed the opinion that

Mr. Waite is the most determined and possibly the only energetic member of the party; that Mr. Piper is the most mercurial, quick-witted and intelligent one, and that Mr. Harrison is the most observant and docile. Mr. Waite, therefore, would soon become restive under my domination and leadership; Mr. Piper would wish to pit his wits against mine and might therefore put the success of our enterprise in jeopardy; so, on all counts, I choose Mr. Harrison."

"Thank you, ma'am," said Harrison.

"Shame!" said his companions.

"Please get into my car, Mr. Harrison," pursued Mrs. Bradley. "And, Mr. Waite and Mr. Piper, good-bye." She waved a gloved claw out of the window when she had got back into the car and Waite and Piper drove past. "And now, George," she said to her chauffeur, when the other car was out of sight, "back to Merlin's Castle."

George drove on, to find a suitable place in which to turn the car. Harrison lay back and closed his eyes. In two minutes he was peacefully asleep. Mrs. Bradley prodded him awake again. He smiled at her.

"I'm glad you picked me," he said, and closed his eyes once more.

"So am I," said Mrs. Bradley. "Stay awake just long enough for me to tell you what I want you *not* to do. I don't want to give you any lead whatever in recognizing this so-called manservant, but I am going to take you on a round of visits. If you *do* at any time recognize him, please do not betray the fact until we are out of that person's presence."

"Right, but don't *rely* on me to recognize him."

"You don't need me to labor the point, I know, but the more surprised you are when you discover the identity of this man, the less must you let the cat out of the bag. What you tell me won't be incontrovertible evidence, of course, but I shall believe you implicitly and shall be able to go to work, with the police, upon what you are able to say."

"I see. I'm glad we shall be working with the police. It sounds so nice and safe."

"Physically, that is about the last thing it will be, child. Our man is alert and cunning, and a very cool customer, I fancy."

"Well, if he's the murderer, he must be. He walked right into us in that unexpected way, and didn't turn a hair."

"So I have gathered."

"Do *you* think he's the murdered?"

"It is still only surmise on my part, but I think there were two. Now you may sleep if you wish."

But Harrison did not sleep. He stared calmly out of the window and wondered when and whether he would get any dinner that evening. Except under strong compulsion, he was a law-abiding creature, and was relieved that the lot had fallen to him of being on the side of the angels for the first time since he had been shown Professor Havers' ridiculous advertisement in the newspaper.

"I say," he said diffidently at last, "I'm not trying to get hold of any secrets, but from what you say I imagine you've a pretty good idea of who that manservant really is."

"I have, child, and I shall be very much surprised if I am wrong."

"But you don't think he committed *both* murders?"

"If one man committed both murders, then I have not the slightest idea what man he could be. But if there were two murderers, then one of them must be the man I have in mind."

"Yes, I see. And suppose I pick somebody who isn't the man you have in mind?"

"Then my theory falls to the ground and you will be able to rejoin your friends in further nefarious enterprises."

"Really? Then . . . no, I said I wouldn't try to worm things out of you, and I won't. I say, you know, I'm clumsy at expressing things, but you do realize how absolutely grateful . . . I mean, it would have been dashed awkward for us if we'd been jugged as the persons who appeared first on the scene, you know."

"In the case of Professor Havers, I think you did appear first on the scene, although you did not see the body then. In the case of Mr. Aumbry, you could not have done."

"Well, of course, there *was* that somewhat mysterious caller who turned up after Peter had gone for the police. I suppose they haven't found out who he was?"

"No, they haven't found that out, but I think I might hazard a guess."

"The murderer returning to the scene?"

"No. I think it was Mr. Frederick Aumbry, who, having lost his uncle's hundred pounds at Goodwood, had returned to Merlin's Furlong with the intention of borrowing one of his uncle's treasures in order to pawn it."

"Sorry; I don't follow." Mrs. Bradley explained by describing her interview with Frederick, and by adding what she had learned (from the inspector) of Frederick's very weak alibi.

"Oh, I see," said Harrison. "I suppose we gave him rather a shock."

"I have no doubt you did; and he could scarcely report your activities to the police without giving some explanation of his own presence on the premises."

"Yes, I see. I wonder whether each of the nephews had a key to the house? It seems a bit odd if they had."

"I doubt very much whether they had. Frederick is an ingenious man, however."

"Oh, you mean he must have sneaked the keys at some time and had them copied. It would be simple enough. I say, I'm awfully hungry! Do you think I could dine you somewhere?"

"Of course. But before we go any farther there are two things I'd like to ask. The first is to enquire whether you realize that to nearly all your questions I have returned an evasive answer."

"No, I didn't realize that."

"Think it over, Mr. Harrison. Have you a good verbal memory?"

"No, I don't think I have. I never could learn things by heart, if that's what you mean."

"That is not quite what I mean, but never mind. The second is this: how did you three men come to find the way to Merlin's Fort instead of to Merlin's Castle or Merlin's Furlong?"

"How did we? I don't really know. The porter misdirected us, I suppose."

"Yes, but you had a map."

"The Castle and the Furlong weren't marked on it by name."

"But Merlin's Fort was, you know."

"Yes, but we weren't thinking of Merlin's Fort. You know how it is with a map. On the whole, one only looks for the place one wants to get to."

"I see that very clearly, of course. Having arrived at Merlin's Fort, exactly what did you do?"

"I collared the back seat of the car and our only rug, but the others swiped the rug and went off a few hundred yards and camped out, in the heather. I thought you'd been told all this. We told the police."

"And next day you came to Merlin's Castle."

"Yes, after a bit. But it's been proved that old Havers was dead before we got there. He'd been killed on the previous night while we were at Merlin's Fort."

"You were all in the neighborhood, though, weren't you?"

"Yes, but we didn't know then that such a place as the Castle existed. It was the Furlong we were after."

Mrs. Bradley wagged her head.

"I think you are hungry, are you not? Let us dine, and, while we dine, you must give me all the latest news of my nephew, Bradley of Angelus."

CHAPTER ELEVEN

Merlin's Treasure

"Yea, slimy things did crawl with legs
Upon the slimy sea."

S. T. Coleridge—*The Ancient Mariner*

An early dinner in Moundbury ministered to Harrison's needs and caused him to refrain from asking Mrs. Bradley the question which was uppermost in his mind. She guessed what it was, and, as soon as they were on their way again, she put it to him directly.

"You are wondering why I said Merlin's Castle, which is empty, when I must have meant Merlin's Furlong where various persons not unconnected with our matter, are, or have recently been, in residence." Harrison admitted that such a thought had been in his mind. "It's the diptych," she continued. "Nobody else appears to have remembered, but the fact remains that, but for the diptych, the expedition of the Three Wise Men of Gotham would never have been undertaken at all."

Harrison agreed.

"Curious that we didn't find it," he said. "It makes me wonder whether old Havers was . . . well, to put it mildly . . . havering when he put that advertisement in the papers."

"No, I certainly think he had lost the diptych, although it seems possible that he gave it away. This means that the theft of the diptych may or may not have been a fact, but the wording of that extraordinary advertisement which was put in the newspapers about the doll no longer gives rise to any doubts."

"Would you care to explain what you mean?"

"I *could* explain very easily, but I mustn't bias you, or your help will not be as valuable as I had hoped."

"I see. May I ask what we do when we get to Merlin's Castle?"

"Yes. We look for the diptych . . . not that we shall find it. If we do I shall be very much surprised. And then . . ."

"We did have quite a look for it when we were there, you know, before we discovered that it was Havers' own house, and not Aumbry's. Do you mean that Mr. Aumbry's murderer took the diptych before we arrived, and returned it to Merlin's Castle? But why should he do such a thing?"

"I don't think he did. But now," she added, "here we are." She picked up the speaking tube. "Find a place by the roadside where you can park, George,

105

and stay at the wheel. Mr. Harrison and I will proceed, by devious and probably illegal means, to force entry into that house at the end of the drive which
we are approaching."

"Here, I say!" protested Harrison. "No more cat-burgling for me!"

"Nonsense!" said Mrs. Bradley firmly. "Besides, we will knock at the door
first. Then, if the castle is empty . . . that is to say, if the police have given up
their tenancy, and I expect they have by now . . . well, you know the way into
the long gallery and can admit me by the back door or some other such
innocuous portal. Don't be a coward."

Feeling like a puppy about to be given an unwanted bath, Harrison shivered with apprehension, but obediently walked with her to the Castle gate.

"Childe Roland to the dark tower came," said Mrs. Bradley with ghoulish
and misplaced enthusiasm. Harrison groaned dejectedly.

"It's a jolly good thing you're in with the police," he muttered. Mrs. Bradley cackled, a harsh but happy sound, and quickened her steps. Two great
peals of the front doorbell produced no result whatever, and a moment later,
while his genius and tormentor kept careful watch, the wretched Harrison
repeated a previous and most unlucky feat and swarmed up onto the porch.
Mrs. Bradley waited until he was in by means of the broken window and
then, with a last look round, she retreated to the obscurity of a shrubbery and
worked her way round to the back. Harrison let her in and was left on guard
whilst she conducted her own explorations.

She went first to the principal bedroom. As she entered there was a scrab-
bling sound followed by indignant and frightened chattering, and a small
monkey shot up the dusty window curtains and sat on the curtain pole gib-
bering down at her.

"But you're not in the police files," said Mrs. Bradley, peering up at it.
"How do you come to be here? Are you a friend of the two who have now left
the house?"

Watched anxiously by the nervous and semi-human creature, she made a
quick search of the room. There was only one startling feature. When she
opened the door of a deep and built-in cupboard she thought at first that she
had discovered Bluebeard's original chamber, for, facing her, was a row of
heads hanging from hooks by their hair. These, however, were only the heads
of dolls.

"Pretty ideas some people seem to adopt," she said conversationally to the
monkey; for round the neck of each of the exhibits was a splash of red paint
as though the dolls had been living persons once, and had been decapitated.
She wondered whether this could have been one of Professor Havers' morbid fancies, but decided that, whether it had been or not, somebody else must
have hung the dolls' heads in the cupboard or the police would surely have
made some mention of them.

She closed the cupboard door, delved into her skirt pocket and produced a bit of nut chocolate. Then she chirruped agreeably to the monkey.

"Here you are. This is for you," she said, as she placed the chocolate on the window-seat. She went out, closing the door behind her. Next she tried the long gallery from which the patient, obedient, desperately fearful Harrison was still keeping watch.

"No luck?" he asked.

"One small monkey and a cupboardful of decapitations only," she replied with a mirthless grin.

"What?" demanded Harrison, incredulously.

"Go and look, if you don't believe me."

He gave her a long stare, decided that she was serious, and went to see for himself. The monkey came down the curtains like a flash, picked up the chocolate, flew at Harrison and, darting up him, stuck the chocolate between its jaws and grabbed his hair. His cries brought Mrs. Bradley to the rescue.

"Really, Attila," she said sternly. The monkey gave a cry of terror and leapt for the curtains again. Harrison rubbed the top of his head, and, eyeing the monkey apprehensively, went to the cupboard.

"Oh, ah?" he said. "Yes. I see what you mean. Those weren't here when we came before, I can assure you of that."

"So I supposed," Mrs. Bradley replied. "The question is, who put them there, and why."

"You don't think they have any bearing on the murder?"

"Answer your own question."

"Oh, I see. Yes, well, there's no doubt a doll began it all, so far as we were concerned."

"A fact we should keep in mind. And now, I think, you should perhaps return to your post."

As soon as he was on the watch again Mrs. Bradley went to the table in the long gallery and took out various envelopes. They did not help her. Beyond establishing what she knew already, that Merlin's Castle had undoubtedly been the country residence of Professor Havers, there was nothing more to be gained from them. They certainly gave no clue to the identity of his murderer. The professor appeared to have been a methodical man, for every bill had enclosed with it its receipt for payment.

Mrs. Bradley put everything back exactly as she had found it, and then sat down in the swivel chair opposite the desk and gave her mind to the solution of the problem. The gallant Harrison, having received no further orders, remained where he was, on watch.

"Really," said Mrs. Bradley, contacting him twenty minutes later, "one begins to wonder whether there is any such diptych at all." She did not mention that she had not even troubled to look for it.

"I know," agreed Harrison gloomily. "And I'm getting tired of the view."

"Poor child! But bear with me for a little. There must be some answer to the riddle. Let me see, now. The body was found in the coach-house. Let us repair thither, and work back again from there."

Harrison, who found a strange comfort in her presence, readily agreed, and together they descended the ornate and noble staircase, and Mrs. Bradley led the way to the rear of the house. The coach-house did not belie its name. It was a stone-floored outbuilding lighted only by a skylight. Its atmosphere was dank and chilly, and there seemed to be no doubt that it had never suffered the indignity of having been turned into a garage. It was agreeably furnished with three great armchairs, a settee and several smaller chairs. There was no table, but in the center stood a large square block of marble, a compromise, Mrs. Bradley suspected, between a butcher's slab and an altar. But the main objects of interest were the effigies of a cat and a parrot which stood on a high shelf above the double doors.

Harrison was interested and alarmed.

"I wish the cat didn't remind me of Waite," he observed.

"Cats and parrots are all very well in their way," said Mrs. Bradley, "but what we find is a monkey. Give me your observations upon that."

Harrison grinned.

"I could make lots of observations," he remarked. "The wretched thing bit me. I would hate to tell you what I said when that happened, and what I could say even now."

"You have my sympathy, dear child. But what do you make of all this?" She waved her arm around to indicate the coach-house and its peculiar, not to say curious, decorations. Harrison sniffed the air and looked dubious.

"Metaphorically a nasty smell," he replied.

"I agree. And this is where Professor Havers' body was found, and between the deaths of Professor Havers and of Mr. Aumbry there was only a very short time. Who else besides the professor himself knew that you were going to Merlin's Furlong for the diptych?"

"Nobody, as far as I know. Of course, the black servant girl could have listened at the keyhole, but I should have thought that the professor's references were pretty obscure, you know; and I'm afraid both of us . . . Peter and myself . . . were more or less playing the fool. I shouldn't really think she could have gathered what was in the wind unless the professor had previously tipped her off, and that doesn't seem very likely."

"I agree. It doesn't seem likely at all. The chances, then, are in favor of the notion that nobody except the professor and your three selves knew of the proposed expedition. Well, I think we've seen everything here that is likely to help us. Let us on to Merlin's Furlong."

"What about the monkey? Won't the wretched beast starve?"

"I doubt it very much. He seemed well-nourished."

"Then, you mean, somebody comes here every day?"

"Well, somebody feeds the monkey, and somebody put those dolls' heads in that cupboard."

"But who could it be?"

"I will hazard a guess. I think it might be Bluna's young man, given previous orders."

"But wouldn't he be afraid of Havers' ghost?"

"He would be more afraid of not carrying out Havers' instructions, I imagine. Never mind. Both the parrot and the monkey are safe."

They were soon at Merlin's Furlong. The police had done with the place, and so, apparently, had Mr. Aumbry's nephews, for it was deserted, and they pulled at the gatehouse bell for half a dozen times in vain. Harrison gazed up at the twin towers.

"I suppose everything is locked up," he observed. "Any point in my trying to break in?"

He sounded so half-hearted in making this suggestion that Mrs. Bradley laughed.

"No," she said. "Why should we trouble when here comes somebody who will admit us?"

Harrison swung round. A small car had turned into the drive. It drew up and out stepped Frederick Aumbry. If he was surprised to see them he did not show it. He raised his dark green hat, brushed down his small mustache and greeted Mrs. Bradley cheerfully.

"Want to go inside again?" he asked. "We all packed up as soon as Godfrey and Lewis had gone through the old boy's papers. Nothing very interesting, I'm afraid. I've been over to see Richmond. The poor old chap is very down in the mouth, but I think I've cheered him up quite a bit by referring to your capacity for getting the right person hanged. "If Mrs. B. is on your side, you've nothing to worry about," I told him."

"Thank you," said Mrs. Bradley. "I came to see that hole in the floor of the Queen's Bedroom which, you remember, you described to me."

"Oh, ah? As a matter of fact, I went over to old Rickie to find out whether he'd permit me . . . Rickie being the heir, don't you know . . . to do a spot of investigating there myself. He agreed, so long as I took along the boodle to the police to see whether they recognized any of it as stolen property. 'I don't want to be charged with grand larceny if the murder charge fails, by some miracle, to materialize,' says the old lad. So here we all are, and can witness to one another's findings. I see you've brought your own witness, anyway. Jolly sensible, if I may say so. I ought to have thought of one for myself."

Mrs. Bradley introduced the two men, and then Frederick produced keys and soon they were all three climbing the stair which led to the room which the three undergraduates had visited first in their tour of Merlin's Furlong, and from which led the passage into the occupied rooms along the courtyard.

"Interesting old bed," observed Frederick, who, if he had hoped to remove something from his late uncle's hoard for his own benefit, was putting a very good face on things. "The hangings are made from tapestry supposed to have been worked by Berengaria of Navarre. It really *does* belong here . . . unlike some other things I could mention!"

He turned towards the middle of the floor-space and took out a small screw-driver. The worn carpet was soon up and pulled aside, and the trap door opened. It had covered a cavity about three feet deep.

"Surely," said Harrison, peering in, "there's some indication downstairs of the existence of this thing? There must be a drop in one of the ceilings the size of a biggish cistern!"

"Ah, that's where the old boy was clever," said Frederick, prostrating himself on his stomach and reaching down into the hole, which appeared to be absolutely empty. "I'll show you. I found this out by accident. It's very nibby. Very nibby indeed. The old chap used to keep a selection of silverware in the top part. Good stuff, you know, but nothing that couldn't be matched in a couple of hundred old houses, if not more. Then, under the silver, there was this. It goes down to an ancient guard-room, long since bricked up from outside."

His groping fingers produced a sudden result. There was a slight click, and then what appeared to be the floor of the hole slid away to the left and disclosed another hole, very much deeper than the first.

"I'd better go first," said Frederick. He rose, dusted himself down, and then climbed into the hole. Apparently there was a wall-ladder, for gradually his body began to disappear and at last from the depths came a click, and Harrison, who was lying flat with his head over the hole, and Mrs. Bradley, who was squatting like a toad beside it, saw a light come on and then Frederick's face looking up at them from a drop of some twenty feet. "You can come down now," he said. "The trap door is not very big, but there's plenty of room down here."

Harrison had once visited a Neolithic flint mine. Old Mr. Aumbry's trea-sure-house was, to his mind, rather similar. The narrow descent widened at the bottom into a room about eighteen feet by ten, from which three narrow passages opened out. He stared around him with interest. The room was shelved like a wine cellar, and on every shelf was an assortment of objects which, for the most part, would rarely be matched outside a museum or those treasures still in the possession of the Church.

"Pretty, aren't they?" said Frederick. He picked up a jeweled miter in one hand and an ivory Madonna in the other. Putting them down and moving on, he lifted up the gold top and crook of a pastoral staff and a fourteenth-century chalice. In fact, so far as Mrs. Bradley could see, every one of the precious objects in Aumbry's hoard had some religious significance. She mentioned this to Frederick. He agreed at once.

"Yes, quite right," he said. "Makes the things very difficult to pawn. Besides, I imagine that most of them would be on the police list. It beats me how the old devil got away with all this red-hot loot."

"But you thought he was a receiver of stolen goods in another sense," said Mrs. Bradley.

"Well, one was bound to think so. The secrecy, the queer coves he used to do business with, this cover of his at Wallchester, affecting to be a learned crank but one quite above suspicion . . ."

"He must have been learned, in a sense," put in Harrison, "if this was his idea of a collection of valuable objects."

Frederick moved on without replying. It was clear that he was wondering how soon he could get rid of them. Mrs. Bradley loitered, ostensibly examining the collection with the eye of a connoisseur, but, all the time, keeping Frederick under scrutiny. Suddenly, as Frederick, on the opposite side of the room, was weighing the respective merits of an ivory carving of the late fourteenth century, a fifteenth-century pendant, and a large, jeweled brooch of the same period, she stretched out a yellow claw and picked up an old leather handbag. She opened it and, not to her surprise, found that it housed a gold and enamel diptych. What interested her was that it was accompanied by a watchmaker's eyeglass. She slipped both articles into her skirt pocket and put the leather bag back into its place. She thought that Frederick Aumbry sighed with relief.

"But how on earth did you guess?" demanded Harrison, when they were driving off, leaving a satisfied Frederick in possession to loot the hoard as he pleased.

"I thought it might be worthwhile to contact Frederick Aumbry, the human jackdaw," Mrs. Bradley replied.

"You mean we met him by design, not accident?"

"Quite so, child."

"Then we need not have gone to Merlin's Castle? We were just killing time until Aumbry was due to turn up?"

"Not at all. I wanted to visit Merlin's Castle at a time when I guessed it would be empty."

"Except for that beast of a monkey!"

"Except for that beast of a monkey."

"But what about this Negro who looks after it?"

"If he had been there I should have produced my police permit."

"Oh? Have you got one?"

"False, of course, but it would deceive the casual and possibly frightened observer. My secretary effected it. A capable girl with a very strong sense of humor."

"So Frederick had the diptych after all! But how did you know?"

"I didn't know, but I put an advertisement in the Personal column of *The Times,* asking Frederick (no surname, of course) to meet me outside the Ministry of Fisheries and giving the time. I added that he should bring uncle's snuffbox with him as I wanted to show it to Roberts."

"Polly ought to take your correspondence course," said Harrison.

"He has no need to do so. I very much admired the advertisement which brought you to Professor Havers' lodgings in the first place."

"But Havers wrote that himself!"

"Did he? I take leave to doubt it. It is true that I have not seen very much of Mr. Waite, but I admire (without liking) his sense of the macabre."

Harrison laughed uncertainly.

"Polly's pretty good fun," he said. "Did he *really* word that advertisement himself and stick it in the paper? But, if he did—I mean, old Havers didn't turn a hair when we two blew in, you know."

"No. He badly wanted to get rid of that doll," said Mrs. Bradley. "It was sufficient warning."

"Then you mean it *didn't* represent Aumbry?"

"From what I saw at Merlin's Castle in Professor Havers' room, I should say that it represented *him* in the clothes he sometimes put on in the country."

"But the doll wore a little Imperial."

"The doll wore a goat's beard, child. I have examined it carefully. That was not human hair."

CHAPTER TWELVE

Merlin's Cat

*". . . there had been something more than acquaintance between them,
as the gift of a necklace shows . . ."*

HELEN SIMPSON—*The Spanish Marriage*

The road to Merlin's Fort seemed shorter than Harrison would have believed possible. He had spent the night in Moundbury; Mrs. Bradley with friends she had in Blandford. At ten o'clock next morning they met by appointment at the Seven Stones circle along the road which led to Merlin's Castle, but the car, driven by Mrs. Bradley's man George, soon bumped its way off the road and took a long and seemingly endless turning at the end of which could be described, from far-off, a lofty and imposing hill.

"Yes, that's it," said Harrison, "and here's where we met that fellow who misdirected us. Well, at least, no, perhaps it's not fair to say that. He did his best, I suppose."

The car bumped on and came to rest on a patch of turf below the frowning heights of the Iron Age fort. Mrs. Bradley and Harrison got out, and George turned the car.

"Now," said Mrs. Bradley, "for the most curious part of our adventure." Harrison, who, for some time, had felt himself bewitched, made no reply, but followed her up a steep slope to where one of the entrances to the fort showed a trench the width of a farm-cart between two enormous bastions of earth. Behind the bastions ran a deep, wide ditch which was filled with sinister shadow.

"Queer sort of place," said Harrison, following his guide up an incline which turned off to the right and led to a concealed entrance to the inner ramparts of the fort. His observation was just, for, even in broad daylight, the place had a morbid fascination. As they penetrated deeper among the prehistoric Iron Age defenses, although the sun shone brilliantly on all the surrounding country, not a single ray appeared to illumine the vast, incredible walls and the deep, steep, stone-lined ditches.

The entrances, all concealed, led further and further into the intricate fort, winding first one way and then another past rampart upon rampart.

"Well, the builders of concentric castles had nothing on these blokes," said Harrison, when at last they had penetrated to the heart of the stronghold and found themselves on a plateau of virgin turf. "What are we aiming for now? The spot marked with a cross?"

"Yes." She took out a pocket compass.

"View was from the north," said Harrison, helpfully. "From where we parked the car that night, I mean."

"And where two slept in the heather," said Mrs. Bradley. She put away the compass and they made their way over the wide stretch of what had been cattle pasture in the time of Iron Age war to where, in the turf, was an unexpected feature, a maze made of baulks, flat on the ground but of obvious intricacy and cunning. Harrison, obeying a childish, comprehensible impulse, began to walk it.

"Hullo!" he said. "Ground been disturbed in the center, and fairly recently, I imagine."

Mrs. Bradley had already noticed the different color of the turf in the middle of the maze. Stepping over the baulks, she approached the patch where the grass was withered, and studied it whilst Harrison continued his perambulation of the seventeenth-century *opus*. The withered patch, from which, it seemed clear, turf had been taken up and afterwards re-laid, measured, so far as she could judge (and her eye was accurate), about eight feet by five.

"How handy are you with a turfing iron?" she enquired of Harrison. He stood still, stated, "I think I've walked half a mile already," and then answered that he had never handled one.

"Disgraceful!" said Mrs. Bradley cheerfully. "When you have completed your exploration of the Minotaur's den George will drive us to a shop in Moundbury where tools may be obtained on payment of the requisite sum, and you shall learn, under his expert guidance, a useful and interesting art."

"There's no such thing as a useful art," argued Harrison, continuing his peregrination, or, as Mrs. Bradley saw it, his pilgrimage. "If it's art it isn't useful, and if it's useful, it isn't art."

Mrs. Bradley invoked the shades of the Union Debating Society and ignored the gambit. She retired to the edge of the maze and seated herself on the short Downland grass. From where she sat she could see the ground-plan of a Roman temple and near it some rough fillings of what she supposed had been recently-excavated storage pits of the Iron Age village when it had had to retire to this stronghold because of danger below. Patiently she sat and brooded upon old, unhappy, far-off things and battles long ago until Harrison, skipping like the ram under whose sign he had been born, leapt from baulk to baulk and came to join her.

"We needn't go at once, need we?" he asked. "Couldn't we walk all round this place and count the tumuli outside it? I'll collect disc barrows and you can have bell barrows, and that's rather chivalrous of me because you'll find lots more of yours than I shall of mine. We ought to be able to spot them for miles from up here."

Engaged in this simple, satisfying occupation, they encircled the fort, and returned, after a long walk, to the entrance by which they had come in. They drove slowly to the main road and then swiftly to Moundbury, where George, who seemed to have an instinct in such matters, took them without loss of time, or any retracing of his route, to a shop which sold every type of gardening implement and agricultural machine. Two turfing irons and a stout spade were acquired, and then Mrs. Bradley rang up the Chief Constable.

"Have you any objection to my taking up about forty square feet of turf on the top of Merlin's Fort?" she enquired. The Chief Constable replied in a doubtful tone that it was the Office of Works' pigeon. "Oh, I'll be sure to put it back," she blithely promised. "Who has already done all that, and recently? Do you know?"

The Chief Constable disclaimed any such knowledge, begged her not to get him into trouble, bade her good-bye, and rang off, and she rejoined Harrison and her chauffeur grinning with hideous cheerfulness. They lunched and then drove again to Merlin's Fort. They waited in the car whilst a shepherd descended with his flock and a couple of hikers concluded their picnic meal and moved off, and then, George carrying spade and a turfing iron and Harrison the second turfing iron, they penetrated the fastness once more and in due course arrived at the maze.

The turfing iron, to Harrison's relief, proved simple to manipulate, and after some manful work the withered turf was all removed, and, whilst he sat down beside Mrs. Bradley and wiped the sweat from his face and neck, George busied himself in a practical, accustomed manner with the spade and burrowed into the meager depth of soil and the rubble of chalk beneath it. His spade struck upon wood.

"Careful, George. This is it," said Mrs. Bradley.

"What is it, madam?" enquired George, resting for a moment from his labors.

"I don't know, but it's possible that it's a coffin. Probe about a bit. Here, we might as well help you. These will do, at a pinch." She picked up a turfing iron, Harrison seized his, and whilst George stood aside until the size and nature of the find should be disclosed, they delicately slid aside the rubble. A modern coffin was disclosed. Mrs. Bradley laid aside her turfing iron, squatted down, and rubbed away the chalky film which covered the small brass nameplate.

"Good Lord!" exclaimed Harrison. "It's young Catfield! How the devil did he get up here?"

"I can guess," said Mrs. Bradley. "But to work, that the dust be once more equal made by the poor crooked scythe and spade. *Not* quite a quotation!"

By the time that they had finished, the place presented nothing markedly different from its previous appearance. George and Harrison, with ruthless, masculine shoes, stamped on the contiguous edges of the turves until even the meticulous chauffeur was satisfied that they could do no more to restore the *status quo* of the strange, unlawful grave. In silence they returned to the road and it was not until they had reached the end of the bumpy trackway that Mrs. Bradley caused George to pull in on to the grassy edge and Harrison to tell the story that seemed to set the seal on Professor Havers' villainy.

"But Polly and Peter know more about it than I do," he concluded.

"We must contact them, and anybody else who can add to our knowledge. And, George, you are interested in gardening and are knowledgeable about such things as grass . . . how long ago was that turf removed and put back before we touched it, would you say?"

"A matter of twenty-four hours, madam, in my opinion."

"I thought the same. These are deep waters, and we must navigate them to the best of our ability. How long will it take you to get in touch with your friends, Mr. Harrison?"

"I can do it as soon as I get back to the hotel, and, if I know anything about them, they'll be here to-morrow."

"Not here. Ask them to meet us for lunch at the *Bell* in Wallchester, and then we can all go together and find out why there has been no report about the disturbing of a grave."

"Catfield wasn't buried in the churchyard, but in the grounds of his own house, I believe," said Harrison. "And I believe he was an orphan and lived with an elderly relation of the same name."

"I see. Have you any idea where we can find this elderly relation?"

"No, I'm afraid I haven't, but I expect Waite would know. He seems to know everybody's business."

Mrs. Bradley noticed that he no longer referred to Waite by his nickname of Polly.

(2)

The village, its name supplied by Waite, proved to be called Titmouse. George purchased an ordnance map and announced, after a brief glance, that he thought he could find his way. This he did with so much success that it was barely three o'clock when the car pulled up in front of the stone-built post office and he got out to ask the way to Mr. Catfield's house.

"That be Marsh Hanger you be warnten," said the post-mistress. "Straight on tell ee yurs the brook babble, and then take the left-'and turnen, like, and I don't thenk ee can mess et. Great beg 'ouse, and sets etself down, like, en the trees." She eyed him with considerable curiosity but had far too much native courtesy to ask questions. She did, however, come out from behind the grille and follow him to the door to get a glimpse of Mrs. Bradley's car and its occupants before they drove away.

Following her directions George soon found the house. It was indeed embosomed among trees, for tall elms hid it from view. There was a lodge but this seemed to be empty, and the gates were wide open and looked as though they had been so from time immemorial. George drove in and the car slowly followed a curved drive bordered by the elms until the façade of a house appeared. It had a dilapidated, unlived-in look, but that it was occupied there was no doubt, for, as the car drew up, an old man came out on to the terrace and stood waiting.

It had been arranged that Mrs. Bradley should make the first sortie alone, so, while George sat like a statue at the wheel after he had assisted her to get out, and the three young men, reunited, looked on with polite interest, she mounted the steps to the terrace and advanced towards its occupant. He did not move, except to turn towards her, and she had to go right up to him before he made any other acknowledgment of her presence. When she reached him, he said, pushing his head forward and back as though he were a tortoise, which, facially, he somewhat resembled:

"I didn't suggest that they should send a woman! I don't know what things are coming to!"

"You do not subscribe, then, to the theory that the sexes, although complementary, are equal?" Mrs. Bradley enquired.

"Complementary my foot! Equal? Bah!" observed the tortoise. "What good can you do now you've come? Oh, well, we'd better go inside, I suppose."

He was leaning on a stick, and he tapped irritably with it as he led the way through the open front door.

"I don't think, you know, that I've come on the errand you have in mind," said Mrs. Bradley when she had seated herself in the chair he grudgingly offered. She looked round the large and handsome library. It was obviously used as a bed-sitting room, for, in addition to an enormous collection of books and the usual furnishings, there was an old-fashioned, brass-railed bed in one corner, and an old-fashioned wardrobe in one of the fireplace alcoves. Although the day was warm and fine, a fire burnt on the hearth and the old gentleman was wearing a loose tweed overcoat on top of a hairy tweed jacket. A muffler was around his neck and his socks were of thick blue wool.

"Haven't you come from the lawyers?" he asked. Mrs. Bradley smiled, a response which he seemed to dislike. "Well, yes or no?" he demanded.

"Interesting," said Mrs. Bradley, "No, would appear to be the answer. I do not come from the lawyers. I come to inspect a despoiled grave."

"What?"

"A despoiled grave," she repeated. "Can it be without the sphere of your

cognizance that your relative, Mr. Catfield, has been removed from his se-
cure resting-place in these grounds and transported to a hilltop in an adjacent
county?" Waite had been convincing on the subject of Catfield's previous
interment.

The tortoise blinked at her.

"You refer to my grandnephew, the suicidal Catfield?" he demanded. Mrs.
Bradley nodded.

"I imagine so," she responded. The tortoise sighed.

"I knew he would still be a nuisance," he remarked.

"Still?"

"Oh, yes. What did he do at the university? Got himself involved in the
troubles and was liquidated. Be that as it was . . ."

"What troubles?"

"Oh, the Town and Gown rows. They went on in my grandfather's time
and they went on in mine. Do not mention that young man to me. I have cast
him out of my thoughts."

"Did you not love him?"

"Love a boy who got into a mess and killed himself to get out of it? No,
madam, I did not."

"A pity," said Mrs. Bradley. "I have an idea that he did not kill himself. I
think he was murdered."

"By me, madam?" demanded the old man, irritated but not shocked by her
announcement.

Mrs. Bradley considered him carefully, and then shook her head.

"I hardly think so," she replied. "Suppose you tell me about it. All I know
at present is that he formed one of a *coterie* of young men who sat at the feet
of the late Professor Havers, who, according to such evidence as I have in
my possession, was not so much a professor of history as a professor of the
base and disreputable art of necromancy."

"An evil genius, madam!"

"Evil, undoubtedly. Genius . . . I don't know."

"May I ask why you have come here, if you're not from the lawyers?"

"Certainly you may. I have come here to inspect the place where first you
buried your relative, and to prove to you that the coffin has been taken away."

"Utter rubbish!"

"Not at all. Let me explain, and, when you have heard me out, I shall hope
to have your co-operation in gaining some further information."

"I promise nothing." He picked up a poker and irritably prodded the fire.
"Besides, I've no time to waste."

"Cannot you spare time to listen while I tell you that your young relative's
body has been conveyed from the grave in which you laid it, and the coffin
taken to the top of a prehistoric earthwork in the county of Moundshire."

"Again, madam, I say it is rubbish!" He replaced the poker as carefully as if it had been made of glass, and turned to face her. His gray old face had expressed disbelief, but this gave way to fury. "Who has dared to tell you such lies!"

"No one. I am reporting upon what I know. Sit down, Mr. Catfield, and listen."

He obeyed her, pushing out his long lips and drawing them in again, and looking, suddenly, a senile, helpless old man.

"Very well," he said at last. "But how can such things be done in a country as well policed as this?"

Mrs. Bradley told him as much of the story of the diptych as served her purpose, and when she had finished and had described the finding of Catfield's coffin, she concluded, "And now I would like you, if you will, to tell me what you know. I am investigating two murders, and I believe young Mr. Catfield's death was a third."

He stared into the fire for some minutes. Mrs. Bradley watched him and waited. At last he roused himself.

"Suicide. His suicide. His disgraceful suicide. Dis<u>honor</u>, corruption, and then death. My grandnephew had feet of clay."

"He was certainly led astray."

"But I tell you . . . No! Why should I lie? All is not quite as you think."

"But I *don't* think," said Mrs. Bradley patiently. "I only want to know. And, surely, for your own sake, and the sake of the family name, it would be better, in a sense, that your grandnephew should have been murdered rather than that he should have died the dishonored death which has so far been attributed to him? Meanwhile, will you give me permission to visit the grave in which you laid him?"

The old man looked doubtful.

"I am what I am," he said. "If I should be that which I follow, then I could not be that which I am. I do not intend to die yet. I will not show you his grave."

"Then may I go and find it for myself?"

He hesitated again, and then raised his hand and pointed. Mrs. Bradley thanked him, and rejoined her three undergraduates . . . or, rather, two of them. Waite, Piper explained, was bored and had gone for a walk. Mrs. Bradley nodded and led the way. They had to pass through a grove of trees in the midst of which stood a small stone altar. It was inscribed in French.

"*Attendez et Voyez?* Crude, surely?" remarked Harrison. "Wait and see. Well, poor Catfield didn't wait here very long."

This observation was justified. Behind the altar, and visible over its flat top, was a hole in the ground which had been filled in only roughly. On top of this inefficient or careless bit of gardening a dead cat had been tossed.

Harrison, who was squeamish, recoiled. Piper picked up a bit of stick and proposed to inter the cat by pushing away some of the light, loose, leaf muld which had been used to fill in the hole; but Mrs. Bradley bent down and studied the cat.

"Dead less than half an hour, I should say," she remarked. "Wait and see. Remarkably interesting. And now, Mr. Piper, if you would be so good . . ."

Piper buried the cat and had scarcely finished his task when old Mr. Catfield appeared on the narrow path through the grove. He came up and looked at the disturbed soil.

"But it wasn't like this when we left him," said the old gentleman. "Who could have done all this?"

Mrs. Bradley had her own answer to this question, but she did not supply it aloud. Silently she accompanied her host to the terrace and there took leave of him.

"What did you gather?" asked Harrison, who had sent Piper in search of Waite to let him know that the party was ready to leave. "Or wasn't there anything to gather?"

"I think there was," Mrs. Bradley soberly replied, "but I did not gather it all because I thought it better not to ask too many questions at one time."

"What didn't you gather?" asked Harrison.

"I did not gather whether old Mr. Catfield had a cat, and, if he had, what has become of it."

"Oh, the dead pussy! By the way (don't harrow my feelings if the answer's horrid), how did it come to die?"

"By manual strangulation, child."

"Good Lord! But . . ."

"No, I can't answer any more questions at the moment. Time for that when you and I have visited Merlin's Fort."

"Merlin's Fort? We don't need to go there again!"

"Don't you want to meet Morgan le Fay, child?"

Harrison said that he was not at all sure that he did, and decided not to ask the question which had come into his head. His knowledge of Mrs. Bradley's mind was not profound, but he felt sure that, to her, Morgan le Fay had another name, a name which he would recognize if he heard it.

Piper came back with Waite, who apologized charmingly for having forsaken the party but claimed a slight previous acquaintance with old Mr. Catfield which he did not wish to renew. Mrs. Bradley accepted this explanation as the truth (which she felt convinced it was) and the quartet got into her car and drove away. She could not help reminding herself, however, that Waite had also preferred not to contact Professor Havers. Waite knew too many people, she concluded, for his own safety.

(3)

The village of Titmouse was within easy reach of Wallchester, and Mrs. Bradley suggested that as she had a standing invitation to visit friends in the north of the city, the three young men might care to go to a cinema or otherwise amuse themselves, and then meet her again at about seven o'clock in the evening. The three were in favor of this arrangement, and the party separated, Mrs. Bradley to ring up the inspector in charge of the case, and the three undergraduates to engage themselves as they would. In answer to her message the inspector turned up with the Chief Constable and Mrs. Bradley's friends put a room at their disposal.

"Begin from the beginning and go on . . . I won't say to the end because the end is not yet . . . but go on to where you think we've got to," the Chief Constable suggested. "Not that I think there can be anything now to upset our own conclusions. We've got the thing pretty well taped."

"We begin," said Mrs. Bradley, "with the nephews of the murdered Mr. Aumbry."

The Chief Constable made no objection to this. In fact, he endorsed it.

"Right. There can't be any doubt about the nephews. As I see it," he said, "we have only two suspects: Mr. Richmond Aumbry and Mr. Godfrey Aumbry; in each case the motive is clear. Unfortunately we have not sufficient evidence to arrest either of these men, and so we are holding our hand. The way we look at it is this: Godfrey believed that he would inherit most of the old man's goods. In a moment of . . . call it whimsy . . . the old man suddenly decided to nominate Richmond as his heir. Before he could change his mind, Richmond killed him and, unless we can prove that he did so, now inherits everything which Godfrey thought of as his own. Godfrey, furious, would have liked to murder Richmond, no doubt, but to do that would not have helped him. While Richmond was alive he could at least borrow from him (we'll say) on the strength of being unjustly dispossessed; he might even be in a position to blackmail him, for all we know. Anyhow, Godfrey had to vent his spite on somebody, so he selected old Professor Havers, of whose malpractices he had known from his uncle. Godfrey had had access, by his own showing, to all his uncle's papers, and there seems to be plenty of evidence that the two old men had been firm friends at one time. What do you say to that? You believe in the sublimation of natural instincts. I suggest that Godfrey sublimated his hatred and disappointment by killing Havers."

"What do I say to it? One thing only," Mrs. Bradley replied. "I say that you must have been able to prove something which I guessed but had no means of proving."

"Good heavens! Don't tell me you'd already tumbled to it!"

"I certainly had, if you mean that the elusive and respectable manservant whom my three undergraduates drove to the station was really Godfrey Aumbry."

"What's more, ma'am, he's admitted it," said the inspector, "but he denies all knowledge of the murder and says that while he was in Professor Havers' castle he did not even see the body."

"If he *didn't* kill Havers, there's just a chance he might be telling the truth," put in the Chief Constable, "because those three young fools don't seem to have seen it either."

"What reason does Godfrey Aumbry give for having been in Merlin's Castle at the time?" Mrs. Bradley enquired.

"Says he had a telephone message from somebody, who claimed to be speaking on the professor's behalf, asking him to go over there, and telling him how to dress. Declares he thought the message genuine, as the professor was known to be a crank if not actually a lunatic, and hoped it was a preliminary to his uncle and the professor making up their quarrel. He was anxious for this, he says, because it might mean he would get the professor's affairs into his hands again. He had lost a client, it seems, when the old men quarreled."

"But you haven't arrested him on suspicion of having murdered Professor Havers?"

"No. We've insufficient evidence to put before a jury. Besides, we want to get Richmond as well. Why did he take in that black girl, Bluna, unless she knew something he wanted to keep secret? Very fishy, you know, that business. I know he explained it by saying the girl had a letter from somebody advising her to apply to him for domestic work, but my guess is that he sent the letter himself. It's all mostly guesswork, so far, I admit, but I do think we're a long step forward now that we've settled the identity of that manservant. It makes quite a story, doesn't it, Inspector?"

"Very good of you to say so, sir. It was only routine, all the same. Nothing like routine for bringing home the bacon. That's what I always say." The inspector assumed a slight smirk of self-appreciation.

Mrs. Bradley's dampening thought, that it was not much good bringing home the bacon if the bacon was already rancid, she did not utter, but congratulated the inspector upon his painstaking work. Then she said:

"A slightly different reconstruction of the known facts would be that Professor Havers murdered old Mr. Aumbry in revenge for the theft of the diptych, and that Godfrey murdered the professor in revenge for his uncle's death which (although Professor Havers could scarcely have known this) deprived Godfrey of his inheritance."

"Oh? So you think *Havers* murdered Aumbry?" demanded the Chief Constable.

"I did not say that I thought so. I was merely offering a theory slightly different from, and, if I may say so, slightly more psychologically sound than, your own."

"But that would let Richmond out entirely!"

"I see no reason why he should not be let out."

"But the motive! It still sticks out a mile!"

"Nothing on earth does that . . . yet. You may be right about Richmond, of course. Everybody has it in him to murder somebody, but I must insist that Richmond would be very unlikely to murder for financial gain."

"Have it your own way," said the Chief Constable good-humoredly. "Another theory, of course, is that Godfrey and Richmond were in collusion over both the murders, but that seems a little far-fetched. But if you don't agree with our conclusions, let us know what you've got up your sleeve."

Mrs. Bradley did not reply that she had nothing up her sleeve.

"I've some way to go yet before I can prove my points," she said, "but there are one or two things to which I can draw your attention. Let us suppose, for the moment, that all Mr. Aumbry's nephews are telling the truth. That, you'll agree, would put a different complexion on everything."

"It would indeed! But why *all* the nephews? We've no reason to suspect Lewis and Frederick, except on the doubtful hypothesis that Lewis killed the old man for his brother Richmond's sake, or that Frederick the Drone killed him for the little bit of cash which he expected to, and does, in fact, inherit."

"Quite," said Mrs. Bradley patiently. "Now then: let me, as you yourself suggested, begin at the beginning. The beginning seems to me to be the death of the undergraduate, Mr. Catfield."

"Suicide. The poor young idiot cut his own throat. We've gone into all that. He was in debt all round at college and dared not go to his uncle for the money."

"Wicked and parsimonious uncles seem to abound in this case," said Mrs. Bradley. "And there is no doubt, as you yourselves know, that the body of young Catfield has been removed from its place of interment and reburied at the top of Merlin's Fort."

"Granted and agreed; and any form of body-snatching is a crime. Go on."

"Next comes the extraordinary affair of Professor Havers' advertisement for some person or persons to restore to him his allegedly stolen diptych, which, by the way, I have found." She produced it and laid it on the table. The Chief Constable picked it up and examined it.

"I wouldn't mind stealing it myself," he said. "It's a unique and beautiful thing. But I'm interrupting."

"That strange advertisement was answered by my three undergraduates, led, I imagine, by the enterprising Mr. Waite, whom I suspect, incidentally, of having worded the thing himself."

"Just his idea of a rag?"

"I doubt it. But, mark this: those three young men had heard rumors of Professor Havers' unsavory reputation."

"You mean they ought to have rumbled him sufficiently to keep clear? That type don't, you know. If the rag seems a bit dangerous . . ."

"Granted. The next point, however, is incontrovertible. In each of the houses which those young men elected to enter, a man was found dead."

"Extraordinary coincidence, I know. But we've been into all that before. You're not inferring that, after all, they were the murderers, are you? Because I just simply don't believe it! Besides, you said yourself . . ."

"I know I did. But I did not know then about young Catfield."

"What's Catfield got to do with it?"

"I wish I knew," said Mrs. Bradley sincerely, "but it is only a matter of time before I find out."

"You and Time seem to be old friends!"

"Alas, yes! It is only Eternity and I who seem to be on opposite sides of the street. But think over what I have said. There are pieces missing in the jig-saw, large and important pieces and also tiny, exasperating pieces, but, although they may be missing, they can't be lost."

"Like the tea-pot," said the Chief Constable. "But go on about Aumbry's nephews. The idea that they might be telling the truth interests me far more than the story of those three half-baked idiots of boys!"

"There you are not altogether wise, but supposing that the Aumbry nephews are telling the truth, we get this: Godfrey, who is not without brains, may have realized as perfectly as his cousin seems to have done, that old Mr. Aumbry, in the end, decided to leave his property to his early favorite, Richmond. You see, apart from anything else, Richmond is the only one of the four who has children. It may well be that the old man wanted to be certain that his wealth would be kept in the family. Family feeling is an extraordinary and powerful emotion. No one can estimate its strength. Even Frederick Aumbry, whom one would scarcely list as a sentimental man, possesses it in some measure. As for the brothers Lewis and Richmond, they are devoted to one another and do not mind everybody knowing it."

"Godfrey's a pretty cold fish, though," put in the Chief Constable, "and if you're right, and the whole four of them *are* telling the truth, we've got to look elsewhere for our murderer."

"Not necessarily; and I am not claiming that they *are* all speaking the truth. I merely wish to assume it for the sake of my argument, which is that not all the factors of this baffling affair can be explained by any theories which, so far, you have put forward. Just let us take the Aumbry evidence in detail, not questioning its veracity, and see what else emerges."

"Well, we can do that, of course. What emerges, however, isn't helpful.

Take Godfrey first, for example. His story begins where he claims to have been hit on the head whilst he was roughing out the draft of a will which was to make him his uncle's heir. His papers were abstracted while he was still unconscious."

"You say that he *claims* to have been hit on the head, but that attack on him has never been disputed. The uncle accused the cousins, and Frederick Aumbry protested, apparently vigorously."

"And Frederick suggested to you that old Mr. Aumbry himself may have crept back into the room and laid Godfrey out. But why should he do such a thing?"

"I think he distrusted everybody, Godfrey (the repository of some of his secrets) most of all. I think we may take it that among Godfrey's papers was a document which made the old man think he was justified in what he had done, and I think we may put the altered depositions partly down to the fact that he thought he had caught Godfrey out in some sort of double dealing."

"So you *really* think the last will, the one in Richmond's favor, was intended to stand?"

"I propose to assume so for the moment."

"But what could Godfrey have found out?"

"For an answer to that question I will refer you to a very interesting sentence in Godfrey's evidence. According to what the inspector has in his notes, Godfrey reported that his uncle said, referring to the special treasure he had promised to show him, "It was the apple of the fellow's eye that had it last." Knowing what we did know, we assumed that he would have been referring to the Isaurian diptych, and that the previous owner was Professor Havers, but has it not occurred to you that he may *not* have meant the diptych, and that, even if he did, the previous owner need not necessarily have been Havers?"

"I hadn't thought like that, but I see your point, of course. The only thing is that, whatever the treasure was, it can't have any bearing on the murder of Aumbry, can it? He can't have been killed so that somebody could gain or regain possession of the diptych, because here it is in front of us, and you found it still among Aumbry's hoard at Merlin's Furlong. That hoard has proved interesting, incidentally. It was, as you suspected, nearly all stolen property, which has now been identified and returned. He must have been a receiver in a big way, and, from what we can gather . . . Godfrey, who went through secret papers which even he had never seen before (or so he says) was our chief informant . . . the old man used to act as fence to the big gangs on condition that they always stole something which he could add to his collection of religious objects."

"Fascinating," said Mrs. Bradley. She rose. "I'll leave the diptych with you. It will be better. There's just one thing before I go to meet my undergraduates." She picked up the diptych and opened it, laid it down again, took from her skirt pocket the watchmaker's eyeglass she had found attached to it, opened a fine penknife, and, screwing the glass into her eye in professional fashion, she delicately inserted the tip of the knife-blade between the inside and the outside of the first of the two panels. There was a very faint click, and the top picture slid aside. Beneath it was a scene of such astonishing obscenity that the Chief Constable recoiled as though a snake had bitten him.

"Good God!" he said.

"Not God, not even the Devil, but merely perverted genius," said Mrs. Bradley. She pushed the little panel into place again, and the plump, imperial features of the Emperor Justinian and the gracious, vacant face of Theodora immediately hid the horrid revelation from view.

"Well!" said the inspector. "And I thought I'd seen a few!"

"Yes," said Mrs. Bradley, some of whose patients had, from time to time, introduced to her notice their collections of *erotica*, "it *is* an interesting example."

"No wonder an old satyr like Havers was anxious to have it back," said the Chief Constable. "I wonder how he came to get hold of it in the first place?"

"That is just the point. Another is that Frederick Aumbry, who stole it, was extremely anxious to get rid of it again. He slipped it back among the treasures while Mr. Harrison and I were there, you know, but one can understand that Frederick was able to blackmail his uncle on the strength of it. The biter bit, in fact!"

CHAPTER THIRTEEN

Merlin's Fort

"With tapers let the temples shine,
Sing to Hymen hymns divine;
Load the altars till there rise
Clouds from the burnt sacrifice."

MICHAEL DRAYTON—*The Fay's Marriage*

Mrs. Bradley did not go back at once to the Fort. She and the three young men went to her house at Wandles Parva and there they told her something of Professor Havers and his iniquities. It did not amount to much.

"There were rumors, you know, as there always are," said Waite, "and some of them weren't too sweet."

"Do not attempt to spare me on account of my age and sex," said Mrs. Bradley. "I know something about most of the sins of this world, and in witchcraft I have always taken interest."

Waite could well believe this. He eyed her intelligently, and then observed: "Did you ever attend a Walpurgis Night?"

"In my own person, no," Mrs. Bradley responded, "but I believe I had an ancestress who did."

"I wish I'd had one like that," said Harrison. Mrs. Bradley shook her head.

"I don't think you do," she remarked. "Consider, Mr. Harrison, and, until you have considered, do not speak. Remember the golden books of Lucius Apuleius, and do not comment upon that of which you have no cognizance."

"Oh, that!" said Harrison, to the astonishment of his companions. "We know all that old stuff."

"We know of it intellectually," said Waite in a tone of rebuke. "We do not know of it personally . . . or do we?"

Piper developed this theme.

"I know what I think," he observed, "and I think on my feet."

"As no true sage has done," said Mrs. Bradley, "from the time of Diogenes onward. Serious thought does not and cannot emanate from the feet, the root of all pain and evil, but from the stomach, wherein reposes the fount of appreciation and the true justification of mankind, likewise his death and damnation."

"But about Havers," said the practical Waite. "I'll admit that most of what I know is merely hearsay, but there's no doubt young Catfield was mixed up in something rather nasty. He was a lonely sort of cuss, and gravitated naturally, I suppose, towards anything sociable. There used to be parties . . . reading parties, they were called . . . held by Havers out of term-time . . . and most of my information comes from a man at St. Swithin's who went to one of them. Havers was at St. Swithin's, you know, and nearly all his devotees came from there. I don't think anything much happened during term except on Midsummer Eve, but most people are pretty busy about then, so not much was noticed, I suppose. This man . . . you don't want his name, do you? . . . I mean, I know he only went to the one and decided, on that, that it wasn't his kettle of fish."

"His name doesn't matter. What put him off, do you think?"

"Well, he didn't care for any of it much. Old Havers appears to have mixed up voodoo and the leopard men with a spot of goat worship, and he procured a few rather disreputable ladies to chuck in for good measure. It appears there were strange and wonderful dances in the lee light of the moon."

Mrs. Bradley did not ask for a detailed description of the revels, and Waite, after a thoughtful pause, turned to Piper.

"Contribution similar," said Piper, "as Polly and I were together at the above recital. It was all, on the surface, a bit childish, you know, and, like lots of childish things (say the bat-eyed righteous what they may), a bit nasty. Anyway, underneath, you may take it, it was foul. This man who took us said he thought drugs were used to induce the party spirit and supply the requisite energy, and there appears to have been some pretty massive atrophy of the pleasanter notions of civilized motivation."

"Yes," put in Harrison. "Havers came in tight (or drugged) to a lecture once, and somebody got him on to his favorite subject by putting an adroit question destined (with the worthiest intentions, incidentally) to divert Havers' remarks from the matter in hand, which was of dim and doubtful interest, to the question of Roman reliance upon astrology. The answer Havers gave, although, in one sense, astonishingly interesting, was also astonishingly rude. Some of the mob thought it staggeringly funny, of course. Personally, I had nightmare after it. Two men, destined for the Church, walked out. The queer thing is that although I 'ad the complete 'orrors, I can't actually recollect a word that Havers said on that occasion."

"And Mr. Catfield?" asked Mrs. Bradley.

"Well, there were rumors that his uncle got to know the way things were moving," said Waite. "There was a school of thought in St. Swithin's that wanted to gag Catfield at night because he used to yell and shriek in his sleep. The inference some of us drew was that he may have done the same thing at home—yelled and shrieked, I mean—and that may have meant that he let a few cats out of bags. Anyway, he was sent down, but he still stayed in Wallchester, apparently, and a fortnight afterwards we heard of his suicide."

Perceiving that the young men would tell her little more, Mrs. Bradley dismissed them to their slumbers, whereon her maid Celestine took it upon herself to observe, as she sympathetically watched their progress upstairs, "Ah, these poor little ones! How one carries oneself grandly in youth, and how one undoes oneself with age!"

Rightly disregarding this sentimental utterance, Mrs. Bradley betook herself to her chauffeur George and suggested that he should drive her to Moundbury.

"For there alone," she said, "and only there shall we come upon the solution of one of these mysteries."

George was interested, and alertly observed:

"The young gentlemen, madam, lacking discretion and experience . . ."

"Not altogether," said Mrs. Bradley. "One of them, at least, does not lack some kind of experience, and although one hesitates to believe that witchcraft still flourishes in the rural districts of southwest England, one's mind, I feel, should never be closed to exclude latent possibilities."

They drove, at Mrs. Bradley's orders, straight to Merlin's Fort. Instinct had not played her false, for at Merlin's Fort strange rites appeared to be in progress. The first inkling that she and her chauffeur had of this was that the landscape seemed to be on fire.

George pulled up on the edge of the Downland turf and helped Mrs. Bradley out.

"Up the side of the hill outside the fort. We can probably see from the top," said Mrs. Bradley. There was a rough path worn by hikers and bounded by a stone wall. She and her man used torches, for here and there the path went up in a series of natural steps formed by outcroppings of the limestone. It was a steep, stiff climb and they did not attempt to hurry.

When they reached their vantage point they could see across the abysmal banks and ditches which guarded the plateau to the source of the devilish illumination which they had been able to see from below. It was caused by a number of flaring and smoking torches which cast a light of orange, brown and red to light about forty dancing figures. Towards the watchers was borne an acrid tang as the torches burnt down lower and their showers of sparks flew more wildly, and across the gulf came the sound of discordant chanting, as though Plainsong were being distorted by the cozens of Evil.

George and Mrs. Bradley watched and listened, and after about five minutes she remarked that she was about to storm the fortress, but would return first of all to the car. They scrambled and slid down the stone or picked their way carefully over the scree, and shortly reached their parked vehicle.

"Splendid," said Mrs. Bradley. "You know, George, I shouldn't be at all surprised to find that all those people had blackened their faces, as poachers and the stealers of Christmas trees often do."

"For an identical purpose, do you mean, madam? In order to escape detection?"

"Yes, indeed, George. This place is remote enough, in a sense, but it is only a mile or two away from a main road, and I don't think the police would take a broadminded view of what has been going on up there this last couple of hours. I wonder . . . but, yes, it must be, unless I have cast the runes wrongly. I have to find someone up there who knew Professor Havers and knew something to his discredit, and if I can catch such a person taking part, or (more likely), having taken part, in the kind of revels which I fancy have been held tonight in Merlin's terrifying fort, I shall be well on the way to solving such mysteries as trouble us."

"Yourself and the police, madam? You refer to the deaths of Mr. Aumbry and Professor Havers?"

"I do, George. And now, I must become the questing fairy."

George, accustomed to the ways of his employer, waited respectfully for orders, being certain that these would embrace an original note. Mrs. Bradley produced a hunting horn and held it in the glow of a headlamp.

"Behold, George," she said. "When you hear this (or *if*, as the case may be) have your engine running, for I shall be like the poor man in the *Metamorphoses*, in the monstrous power of witches. It may be that they 'can call down the sky, hang earth in heaven, freeze fountains, melt mountains, raise the spirits of the dead, send gods to hell, put out the stars,' but, on the other hand, they may more simply (but probably not more purely) be ladies and gentlemen in evening dress who are incapable of concocting even an Irish stew or the dubious alibi of the rissole. Wait, and we shall see."

"Very good, madam; and if . . ?"

"If you do *not* hear the horns of Elfland faintly blowing, I shall be dead, I shall be sped, and my soul (I hope and trust) will be in the sky." She sounded cheerful, but George possessed, to his sorrow, the bump of caution.

"How long am I to allow, madam, before taking appropriate action?"

"If, by appropriate action, you mean climbing into the fort and up to the revels with your heaviest spanner in your hand, you must wait until dawn. In other words, I do not see how to set a time limit while darkness is still upon us. But dawn will shortly be at hand, and, in any case, I confidently expect to remain at large and undetected unless they've put guards in that sunk road which leads to the citadel."

She put the hunting horn back into her pocket, switched on her torch, which she pointed towards the ground, and glided away. Left alone, George got out the spanner and also a small, illegal cosh which his employer did not know he possessed. Then he sat on the step of the car with his face towards the mass of Merlin's Fort, and strained his ears.

There was nothing at all to be heard except the chanting, which was growing throatier, and nothing at all to be seen except the now wildly smoking torches as they wove the patterns of Erebus against the remote night sky.

Mrs. Bradley, whose eyes very soon became accustomed to the thin summer darkness, switched off her torch as soon as she had identified the entrance between the great bastions of turf and stone, and made progress, so that in a comparatively short time she had threaded the maze-like lines of baulks and sunken roads and was on the edge of the plateau.

Here a strange sight met her eyes. Except for three tall figures, the torch-bearers (who apparently were wearying of their task), were tossing down their *impedimenta* and had begun to dance out the flares. Sparks, mingled with squeaks of pain as some rash worshipper submitted bare ankles to the fire, stabbed the night through with hideous but humorous recurrence. Mrs. Bradley watched closely. Triple Hecate's team, holding fresh torches high, sufficiently lighted the scene, and Mrs. Bradley was soon to realize that her prophecy to George had been inspired. The face of every dancer was as black as the entrance to the Shades. There was something else. Although to most of the participants to blacken their faces had been a form either of ritual or disguise, two, at least, were black by nature.

Well satisfied with what she had seen, Mrs. Bradley waited until the three tall torchbearers had plunged their torches out, then she joined the throng, her face, after applications from a little bag of the soot which she had procured from her dining-room chimney before setting out, making her one with the company she had elected to follow down the hill.

When they reached the ruins of the Roman temple she was interested to notice that instead of using the main entrance by which she herself had come in, these people had chosen that on the northwest side where the ramparts, she remembered, were steeper but the defenses, otherwise, not as cunningly planned.

When they were outside the fort and were stumbling down a ramp which brought them to the opposite side of the fort from where Mrs. Bradley had parked her car, she perceived the reason for this choice of an exit, for on the turf were drawn up a couple of motor coaches, each with a somnolent driver at the wheel. As the worshippers crowded in, sat down and began to clean the black off their faces, Mrs. Bradley crept near to the second coach and memorized its registered number. She also took very careful stock of the driver. Then she sauntered round the base of the fort and came in sight of the headlights of her car.

"All satisfactory, madam?" asked George. "I assume so, as I did not hear the horn."

"Except that I've had to blacken my face in order to escape detection, all is perfectly satisfactory, George, so far as I am concerned. It is so satisfactory, indeed, that I am in a position to threaten Bluna and her young man with the police, and to trace the motor-coaches which carried these celebrants to dance round the grave of Mr. Catfield, whose coffin, you remember, you and Mr. Harrison discovered and reinterred. I am also ready for another short conversation with Mr. Richmond Aumbry, and possibly another with the blithe and energetic Mr. Waite, who was driving one of the coaches. And now the hour grows late. Home, George, but spare the horses. I wish to indulge in philosophical speculation and the higher thought. Thirty miles an hour should meet the case, I fancy."

"Meaning you now know all, madam?"

"Meaning I now know half and can guess the rest. But guessing won't do for a jury."

George was sufficiently friendly with his employer to venture a further question.

"Were there orgies, madam, as you supposed there might be?"

"On this occasion I think not. Neither, so far as I could determine, was anybody drunk, but I wonder how many doctors will be called upon to minister to blistered feet tomorrow . . . or, rather, later today . . . and what reasons will be produced to account for the blisters!"

"I thought one should never explain, madam."

"A golden rule, and one which, like all the rest of the golden rules which could make this place an Eden, humanity finds it quite impossible to respect. Mr. Waite must have climbed from his bedroom window and driven fast to get here before us!"

CHAPTER FOURTEEN

Merlin's Emissaries

"I shall attend your leisure, but make haste;
The vaporous night approaches."

SHAKESPEARE—*Measure for Measure*

Although Mrs. Bradley went to bed at the rising of the lark, by ten o'clock in the morning she was dealing with correspondence. Her guests had been in the millpond for a swim, had breakfasted, and, at the direct invitation, not to say command, of Henri, Mrs. Bradley's cook (who hinted darkly of a Lucullan repast disguised under the modern appellation of luncheon), had gone off to walk up an appetite. They had asked, with charm and politeness, whether Mrs. Bradley required them to remain on hand, but for reply she had handed them three ash-plants, a botanist's specimen-case, a pair of field-glasses, a camera and a bull-terrier pup. They took these hints gracefully, and were instructed by Henri to be back by half-past one.

Mrs. Bradley and her secretary dealt briskly with correspondence, and by eleven o'clock Mrs. Bradley had dictated the last letter, tossed the last empty envelope into the waste-paper basket, poured herself and her Laura some sherry, and was retailing with considerable liveliness her experiences of the previous night.

"You might have taken *me* along," said Laura. "Why should you hog all the fun?"

"You get your fun to-day. I want you to go to this address and bring back the negro maid Bluna. I don't care how you do it, but I want her here to-morrow or the next day . . . there is no particular hurry. I've told you who her employers are, but I want you to keep my name out of it. You may experience difficulty in persuading her to come."

"Grand!" said Laura, flexing her considerable biceps. "Any idea whether she bites?"

"I have no information on the subject. You will drive yourself, I suppose?"

"You suppose correctly, ma'am. Well, I must say I didn't anticipate the chance of a toot like this! I'll be off, then, shall I? I can get lunch somewhere on the road. It will be much more peaceful than pigging it here with those three assorted half-bakes you brought along yestreen. Nice lads, but much too young, except Polly Waite, whom somehow I can't abide."

She finished her sherry, declined any more, and ten minutes later a small car shot through the gates and headed for the Winchester Road.

" 'Two of both kinds make up four,' " said Mrs. Bradley pensively to her maid Celestine, who came to take away the sherry glasses and the biscuit barrel.

"Indeed, yes, madame," the Frenchwoman earnestly responded. "Mademoiselle Laura, who is affianced, does she still decline . . . ?"

"To dwindle into a wife? She does," replied Mrs. Bradley, solemnly shaking her head. "But that is not one of the couples to which I was referring. Leaving the resolute Artemis out of the picture, who, in your opinion, is the odd person out?"

"Ah!" A broad, understanding smile transfigured the Frenchwoman's face. "Feminine, says madame? And in the house, young men!"

"No, madame did not say feminine."

"Perfectly I understand, madame. She has three of four. She must make two couples, but not of love or of marriage."

"I note you think they can be separated."

"For Henri," said Henri's wife, "I have the greatest regard. That he is a villain and also ugly, uncouth, ungracious and a glutton, I do not deny. Why should I? *En avance,* then, madame! And do not despair. I bring all your little chickens home to roost."

"I am not certain that Henri would appreciate that."

"Madame amuses herself," said Celestine coldly.

"No, no. There is something I want you to do; something which only you, in this house, *can* do."

"*Vraiment?*" enquired Celestine, suspiciously regarding this compliment.

"I'm not joking. Some time or other . . . tonight, I hope, but it may be tomorrow or the next day . . . Miss Menzies will be bringing here a Negro girl. Now it is reasonable to suppose that this girl, as soon as she discovers that you are a Frenchwoman, will trust you. All Negroes are apt to feel that the English do not entirely lack racial prejudice, a feeling which, in far too many instances, is, unhappily, disgracefully true."

"It is true that the French are the only civilized nation," said Celestine. "*Bien, madame.* What secrets do you wish that I should learn?"

"I want you to find out whether the girl's fiancé is at Merlin's Castle, where Professor Havers was murdered . . . and, if he is, why he tends a monkey there. If you can't find this out, well, nobody can. Be your usual tactful self, of course. Don't frighten her."

Having deployed the two intelligent members of her household in tasks suitable to their respective temperaments, Mrs. Bradley telephoned the police and directed them to Catfield's burial ground. Then she settled herself down with the shapeless and repulsive piece of knitting which (so far as her relatives could perceive) was the permanent obsession of her leisure and was

known by the irreverent members of the family as Aunt Adela's familiar
spirit, and in her mind arranged logically a series of events which might have
led to the murders of Catfield, Havers and Aumbry. That young Catfield had
been murdered she was certain. It might have been ritual murder, which could
connect it with Havers the magician; it might have been murder for gain,
which could connect it with Aumbry the thief. There was a slight chance that
the uncle had had a hand in it if any motive could be established, but so far
there was no reason to suspect him. Nevertheless, if murder had been committed, there remained the fact that old Mr. Catfield had been, so far as was
known (this she had just ascertained from the police), the only surviving
relative.

She lunched with the three undergraduates, invited them to amuse themselves as they pleased during the afternoon, and drove to old Mr. Catfield's
forbidding, uncomfortable house and asked to see its forbidding, uncommu-
nicative owner.

"Again?" he asked angrily when she was shown in.

"I am afraid so. You see, Mr. Catfield, our last interview was, to say the
least of it, inconclusive. Since I saw you I have been again to Merlin's Fort."

"What for?" He looked both menacing and suspicious.

"To watch the vampires dance round your grandnephew's grave."

"You jest."

"Indeed I do not. Tell me all that you know, for you do know something, I
feel certain."

But the old man shook his head. He put out his tongue and drew it in again,
protruded his head and retracted it, shook it again, and said:

"No. No. I know nothing about it. I did not care for my grandnephew. He
disgraced me in every way; first, as a child . . . no courage; second, as a youth
. . . no brains; third, as a young man . . . no character. He consorted with
worthless persons. He wasted my substance . . ."

"Ah, yes, I was coming to that. It has been suggested that your grandnephew had his own fortune, but got into debt."

"Oh, yes, he did," said the tortoise, blinking intelligently. "The first sensible thing you've said. Why do you suppose he had so many friends?"

"Professor Havers and his band of devotees, do you mean?"

"I know nothing of any Professor Havers. I am thinking of a man named
Parrot."

"Parrot?"

"Parrot, madam. I could scarcely be expected to forget a name like that,
especially as the fellow in question was anything but a parrot. No vain rep-
etitions for *him!* An original mind, I imagine, with a powerful influence over
the minds of others."

"An undergraduate, do you suppose?"

"I have no information. My grandnephew always made a crony of him. So much I know, and no more. The fellow only once came here."

"Are you sure he was your grandnephew's friend?"

"I only know, of course, what Dexter told me."

"Dexter?"

"Dexter Catfield, my grandnephew; now, of course, Sinister Catfield, the spy, the toady, the suicide."

"I think you mean Vengeful Catfield, the foolish, the murdered, the betrayed. How was his fortune left?"

"To a dolls' hospital, madam."

Even Mrs. Bradley was taken aback by this, although she did not betray the fact.

"Interesting," she remarked. "Was your grandnephew interested in dolls?"

"In certain dolls, madam."

"As you had brought him up to be?"

"I? Certainly not. My hobby is anthropology."

"Did you contest your grandnephew's will?"

"No, no! There was so little left."

"Did any other relative?"

"Dexter had no other relatives, otherwise I should scarcely have burdened myself with the task of his upbringing."

"Will you give me the address of this dolls' hospital?"

"Certainly. It is in Witchborough." He thrust out and pulled in his head again. A malignant gleam lit up twin emeralds in his heavily-lidded old eyes. "And I hope the dolls eat your heart out and make a monkey out of you, and fill your brains with sawdust, you cursed interfering old zombie!" he concluded. Mrs. Bradley quietly withdrew.

"I don't think I'm popular with old Uncle Catfield, George," she said. "How long will it take us to get to Witchborough?"

"We should scarcely make it today, madam, unless you are prepared to spend a night away from home."

"No, I don't think I'm prepared for that. What do you think, George?"

"I think perhaps a night's rest at home, madam . . ."

"Agreed. Then, tomorrow, perhaps, we can hie us to fresh woods and pastures new."

They returned forthwith to the Stone House at Wandles Parva and were in time to receive the polite reproaches of Harrison.

"I thought you'd gone for good," he proclaimed. "Why didn't you take me with you?"

"For good and sufficient reasons, Mr. Harrison," Mrs. Bradley replied. "Would you care to accompany me to a dolls' hospital?"

"A dolls' hospital?" Harrison regarded her askance. Mrs. Bradley cackled.

"Surely your subconscious mind will make the connection," she suggested. Harrison looked thoroughly alarmed.

"I hope not," he said nervously. "Dolls . . . well, they've had too much to do with this business. But a dolls' hospital! Isn't there something a bit odd about that? I thought hospitals dealt with the living . . ."

"Sometimes the dead."

"Yes, but . . . dolls?"

"Neither living nor dead. And that's where the project becomes interesting."

"Not to me. I've had enough."

"Yes, but why, Mr. Harrison?"

"I don't know."

"How much do you really know about Mr. Waite and Mr. Piper?" asked Mrs. Bradley, sensing that his defenses were breached at last.

"Peter's all right."

"And Mr. Waite?"

"He's a headache," said Mr. Harrison peevishly. "Always wanting to *do* things."

"I'll do, and I'll do, and I'll do," quoted Mrs. Bradley in sonorous tones. Harrison looked startled.

"You don't really think that?" he demanded. Mrs. Bradley shook her head in solemn acquiescence with the view thus naïvely expressed. Harrison looked gloomy. "I know what you mean," he agreed.

"Good," said Mrs. Bradley cheerfully. "Then, at last, we know where we are."

"Do we?" asked Harrison doubtfully.

"Mr. Harrison," said Mrs. Bradley urgently, "remember that you were the person I chose to help me to get at the truth."

"I can't let down Polly and Peter," said Harrison, more doubtfully still.

"No, of course not. Well, would you or wouldn't you like to come and inspect the dolls' hospital with me?"

"I suppose so . . . but why, exactly?"

"You might act as a material witness."

"I don't want to be a material witness. It's a horrible thing to be."

"It's the sort of thing one can't help being at times, unless one has no respect for the truth."

"Forward then, to the dolls' hospital."

"Good. I think it will interest you, you know."

Harrison was not certain of this.

"Where is Witchborough?" he demanded.

"Not so very far from Moundbury, I believe, but George will know."

George did know, and he drove them to it next morning. It was a small, rather drab town not far from the coast, and the dolls' hospital was one of a dozen or so small shops in a street at right-angles to the main one. It bore a large, hideous sign with the caption, *"Bring Poor Dolly to Doctor Ned and He Will Make Her Well."* It had the startlingly blasphemous effect of a large-type Bible text displayed as an advertisement in a tram.

George pulled up and his passengers got out.

"By the way," said Harrison, whom the sign had made thoroughly nervous, "oughtn't we to have provided ourselves with a broken doll?"

"The doll, madam," said George, handing it out from the boot of the car.

"I say," said Harrison, eyeing it apprehensively, "couldn't you have wrapped it up, or something? It's pretty conspicuous like that."

The doll was not, in point of fact, a beautiful object. To begin with, it was naked, and this, together with its staring eyes and long, incredibly flaxen hair, gave it the appearance of a tipsy Lady Godiva. The fingers of one hand were broken off and part of its haunches was missing. It looked as though some cannibalistic child had bitten it.

"Conspicuous and revolting," said Mrs. Bradley, leering at it. "Here, you carry it. I'm much too old for dolls."

"You carry it, George," suggested Harrison, backing away from the treasure. George affected not to hear and returned to the driver's seat. Mrs. Bradley cackled, put the doll under her arm, and led the way into the shop. A man of about sixty, wearing a fez, came out from a room at the back.

"My credentials," said Mrs. Bradley, handing over the doll. The man took it and looked it over.

"You want this doll repaired?"

"What else do you do with broken dolls?"

"Sometimes," said the man, "I throw them away. This doll is not worth my time and trouble. Buy the little girl a new one. Or, if you like, I've several second-hand ones you could inspect."

"Unthinkable! What about the sentimental value of this doll? The child thinks the very world of it."

"Very well. I will do what I can. It will cost fifteen shillings. But if the child is fond of it, how did it come to be in this condition?"

"This doll," observed Mrs. Bradley, twining a strand of Godiva's flaxen wig round a yellow forefinger, "once had human hair and . . ." she lowered her voice to a blood-curdling note after glancing round to see whether anyone else was in the shop (Harrison, in cowardly fashion, had retreated to just inside the doorway), "and *human finger-nails!*"

The man's eyes bulged. He leaned over the counter.

"What are you after?" he murmured.

"Do you know of a doll called *Lamia?*" It means bloodsucker."

The man licked his lips.

"We've done nothing about that. The nearest was one we did for . . ."

"Professor Havers? But that wasn't a doll; it was a stuffed cat—unless you mean the parrot."

"It was . . . he only intended it for a joke."

"Did he? Yet the man died."

"It was nothing to do with the cat. That was just a joke, I tell you! The man was murdered. Mr. Aumbry it was. I read about it in the papers." He seemed to be recovering his poise, Mrs. Bradley noted. "And Professor Havers, he's dead, too," he added with satisfaction. "So there's nothing to be done about *him*."

"Ah, but what about Mr. Aumbry's nephews?" Mrs. Bradley demanded. "They are not to be dealt with so easily."

"His nephews? I know nothing about any nephews."

"When did the black man come here for all those heads? And who painted the marks on their necks?"

"I know nothing about it! No black man ever came here!"

Mrs. Bradley did not query these statements, but she saw that the man had begun to sweat.

"If I were you I'd confide in the police. I'm going to. Almost everything is known, and it's the people on the fringe who'll get caught!" she said. "And don't forget the doll you made for Mr. Waite!"

"Did you get what you wanted?" asked Harrison when they were in the car.

"Enough to confirm what I'd guessed. I've advised our rascally master surgeon to go to the police."

"And will he squeal, do you suppose?"

"That I did not ask, but I think I know. And now, dear child, it is time that you squealed, too. How long have you known Mr. Waite?"

"Oh, no, look here, why must you always pick on Polly? We only began all this for a rag, you know!"

"It didn't end as a rag, though, did it? Besides, I got Mr. Waite's name from old Mr. Catfield. Your friend appears also to have been a close friend of the late young Mr. Catfield."

"But old Catfield couldn't have given you Polly's name! Catfield never spoke of him as Waite."

"No, he spoke of him as Polly, just as you do, but Mr. Catfield senior is old-fashioned. He deduced that as Polly was a nickname it would be undignified to use it, so he referred to Mr. Waite as Mr. Parrot. Now, Mr. Harrison, come clean!"

Meanwhile the lively Laura Menzies, Mrs. Bradley's intelligent and original-minded secretary, was turning over in her thoughts as she drove towards

Wallchester the various methods by which it might be possible to persuade Bluna to accompany her back to Hampshire. Much would depend, she thought, on whether she could see Bluna alone. As it happened, she had more luck than she bargained for. At the bus stop near to Richmond's house she saw a young black woman carrying a shopping basket.

Laura pulled up and said, speaking out of the driver's open window, and chancing her luck that this was the girl she wanted, "Hullo, Bluna. Would you like a lift? Where do you want to go? The market?"

Bluna beamed.

"You're very kind," she replied. "I just miss d'bus, and not another for twenty minutes."

"Righto. Hop in," said Laura, reaching back and twisting open the door. Bluna and shopping basket were soon in the car and, after threading its way through one of the less beautiful parts of the city, the car was soon in the High Street and drawn up outside the market. Bluna got out, and Laura drove off to park the car in a less congested region, but promised to pick her up again with her burdens.

Whilst Laura was enjoying a quiet cigarette in a side street she thought out a scheme whereby Bluna's kidnapping could be safely managed. Then she strolled back towards the market to wait for Bluna and take her to where the car was parked, and stood looking at the shop window by which they had arranged to meet. When Bluna came laden with shopping, Laura took one of the baskets, and when Bluna and the goods were packed into the car, and Laura was threading her way towards Richmond Aumbry's house, she said, with apparent casualness:

"If you want any help and advice, I can take you to someone who'll give it. It's become known what goes on at Merlin's Fort."

Having made this remark, she pulled up at the side of the unlovely but comparatively quiet road along which she had been driving, and turned to look Bluna in the face. What she saw satisfied her. Bluna's lower lip was shaking.

"You mean, d'police?" she managed to ask.

"Among others," replied Laura, carelessly. "Well, what do you say?"

"I never had no hand in nothing, not in nothing at all. I swear it, ma'am!"

"Perhaps not, if you mean the murders, but you were seen there, and your young man, too."

"He's just as innocent as me!"

"Very likely, but you know what it is. If people consort with devils they mustn't be surprised if other people can smell the brimstone on them, must they?"

With this picturesque and pertinent query, she drove on again. When they arrived outside Richmond Aumbry's decrepit and unpainted front gate, she opened the car door for Bluna and helped her out with her parcels. The black girl was a piteous sight and Laura was not in the least hard-hearted. She merely intended to carry out her orders.

"You mean you'll get me kept out of jail?" asked Bluna tearfully.

"We'll have a jolly good try. But you'll have to come along with me and tell us what you know."

"They'll eat my heart if I do!"

"No. We shall see that they don't. Besides, they only eat children's hearts. They wouldn't want to eat yours. Besides, Professor Havers is dead, so you've nothing to fear."

Bluna made up her simple mind.

"Change my afternoon off," she announced, "and come with you after I give Mr. Aumbry his lunch."

"Three o'clock at the bottom of the road," said Laura. "That will give you time to wash up."

CHAPTER FIFTEEN

Merlin's Apostates

"It is also not to be omitted that some wicked women, perverted by the Devil,
seduced by illusions and phantasms of demons, believe and profess themselves,
in the hours of night, to ride upon certain beasts with Diana, the goddess of pagans
. . . and to be summoned to her service on certain nights."

The Canon Episcopi translated by H. C. LEA and quoted by CHARLES
WILLIAMS in his *Witchcraft*

Bluna was downright terrified at the sight of Mrs. Bradley. "That five-pound note was a bad one?" she demanded.

"No, no, quite all right," said the witchlike ancient as Bluna obviously recoiled. "Have no fear of that, or of anything else, Bluna. Tell me everything. I am your friend."

Bluna seemed loath to believe this; so loath, indeed, that Mrs. Bradley got up and said to Laura, "You tackle her, dear child. You know what we want. I will see that our three young friends do not disturb you."

Laura, a psychologist in her way, produced a large quantity of sweets.

"Eat up, Bluna," she said, "and if you've no objection to talking with your mouth full, just take down the back hair and let yourself go."

Bluna began to giggle, almost choked on an acid drop, became sober, and said, in the manner of Jim of the household of Tom Sawyer:

"Ole missus, her make me plenty afraid."

"She?" said Laura in the same idiom. "Just cracks you over the head with her thimble, and who cares for that, I'd like to know?"

Bluna began to giggle again, but sobered down once more when Laura remarked that it was a good day for the wind on the heath. In fact, she looked extremely apprehensive and said defiantly, "Always a wind on Merlin's Fort."

"So I believe. What on earth did you all get up to? . . . You know, the dancing, singing and torches?"

"Dancing? Singing? What for?" asked Bluna vaguely.

"What for? Come clean. I want to know what it's all about. Is it a secret society or something?"

"I don't know. Just for fun."

"It wasn't just for fun," said Laura severely, "otherwise you wouldn't be here. Tell me about Professor Havers."

"No. I'll not tell about him."

"Well, tell Mrs. Bradley, then. Come on. Let me ask her to come in. She'll soon make you talk. She's in with the police, you know, and they're rather interested in the death and burial of a certain young Mr. Catfield. You'd be surprised." But Laura herself was surprised when Bluna agreed to have Mrs. Bradley listen to her story. She had not expected the young maid to capitulate so easily, and she found herself wondering whether Bluna proposed to speak the truth. Then she reassured herself. Mrs. Bradley would soon have the truth out of Bluna. It might not be the whole truth at first, but even that would come in time. She opened the door and said quietly, "She's willing to talk." Then she left the rest to her formidable employer, and settled herself to take notes. Mrs. Bradley wasted no time. To Laura's surprise her first question was:

"How many dolls did Professor Havers make?"

"Dolls, ma'am? Only the one the young gentlemen took away."

"But he didn't make that himself."

"Who made it, then?" asked Bluna. "I thought Professor Havers made it his own self."

"No, you didn't. You know as well as I do where it came from, and you know it came by post."

"I *think*," said Bluna, rolling her eyes, "I think another gentleman sent it to the professor."

"That would not surprise me. You don't care to name him, I suppose?"

"Very wicked man. He'd know how I done told you."

"Cut out the Uncle Tom dialect," said Laura, sternly. Bluna giggled once more. "Tell Mrs. Bradley properly, either in English or French."

"I don't speak French. New Orleans, they speak French. I only speak English."

"Speak English, then, and don't stall, or else we shall think you are lying."

"I don't lie," said Bluna sullenly, "and I don't know anything about the dolls."

"Very well," said Mrs. Bradley. "There was only one doll, and you think a gentleman sent it. Whom did it represent?—Mr. Catfield?"

"I don't know. I never only saw Mr. Havers himself in a suit like that, and only once."

"Very well, Bluna. You may go home now. Miss Menzies will take you in the car."

"You don't want me to tell you about the dancing and the torches?"

"I know all about the dancing and the torches." And Mrs. Bradley, with a glance at Laura, went out.

"Why did they move Mr. Catfield's body from his garden up to Merlin's Fort?" demanded Laura as soon as the door closed.

"I don't know. Ain't nebber moved no bodies."

"Spect I growed," said Laura, in menacing tones. "This is no earthly good. I'd better drive you back."

Bluna got up, looked uncertainly from the closed door to Laura's grim young face, and then sat down again.

"I'd like to tell *some* things," she said. "Other things I've sworn not to tell."

"Unship the cargo, such as it is, then, but, remember, enough is as good as a feast. Be succinct but not vulgar, brief but not crude."

Bluna giggled again, and then began to hiccup.

"Incipient hysteria," remarked Laura. "Hold your breath, Bluna, and think of your absent friends . . . Now, speak. Tell me everything you feel you can. Where does the story begin?"

"It begins with Mr. Magee," said Bluna. "Very funny man who makes dolls."

"Mr. Magee? First name Billy?" asked Laura. Bluna giggled again, sensing a joke but without understanding what it was.

"Initial of Z," she replied, "and lives at the top of Professor Havers' house in an attic all dolls."

"And sometimes at Merlin's Castle, in a cupboard also all dolls," put in Laura, "and sometimes he lives somewhere else, and I know where." Bluna looked at her in horror, and suddenly out came a flood of information. Professor Havers had been a bad man. Even Bluna did not know how very bad he had been until after his death, when Mr. Z. Magee had called her in to help him clear up the professor's belongings. These had included all the paraphernalia, it seemed, of the Macbeth witches, plus some extra ingredients of which Laura had never heard but over which Mrs. Bradley a little later on, shook a deprecating head. Babies had been procured and murdered and the bones of their heads reduced to encalcined flour to be used in unspeakable orgies; zombies had been raised; the witchcraft of darkest Africa had been matched against the rituals of secret cozens of Scandinavian witches; the Black Mass had been discarded as being too childish for serious experiment. Werewolves had fawned upon the professor like family watchdogs, and vampires had toasted him in one another's blood. Ghosts at his command had risen from graves and performed the horrid tasks which he had delegated to them, but he was such a bad man that the deeds he forced upon the ghosts were merely those which were insufficiently evil to merit his own attention. Even the dolls had come to life.

Bluna paused for breath at last. Laura had called Mrs. Bradley in to hear the main part of the monologue. Mrs. Bradley laughed, a bloodcurdling sound, and turned to Laura.

"What do *you* think of it?" she asked. Bluna stared from one of them to the other.

"You don't believe me?" she asked.

"No," replied Mrs. Bradley. "If all this, or even part of it, were true, you would be too much afraid of Professor Havers, alive or dead, to have told us any of these stories. Why did Mr. Catfield have to die? Who killed him? Where are the dolls which Mr. Magee has fabricated?"

"The dolls are nothing," protested the deflated Bluna. "Those dolls are nothing at all."

"Then you will take us to see them."

"I cannot. Mr. Magee, he has them in his shop. I do not know where the shop is."

"Ah, but *we* do," said Laura ghoulishly. "Let's get into the car and go and see them. *I'll* protect you from Mr. Magee. I suppose that name's short for Magician! Or shall I get into the car alone and go and get the police? You know too little and you tell too much . . . too much of the wrong things!"

"I don't want to go and see the dolls," said Bluna, beginning to whimper. Mrs. Bradley sighed, and left Laura to it.

"All right. You'd better have some tea," said Laura, "and perhaps you will think things over. Nobody can hurt you except the law now, and we don't want that. We think you're innocent. Buck up, old thing! Tell the truth and shame the devil, you know! And then we'll turn you over to Celestine. She's a Frenchwoman. She won't frighten you."

(2)

"It is not much I gain, madame," said Celestine, two hours later, when Laura had driven away with Bluna to return her to Wallchester and Richmond Aumbry's house, "but certainly I will recount of it the history."

"Sit down and let's have some claret," said Mrs. Bradley. "Henri, too. There is nothing in the recital which is unfit for his ears, I suppose?"

"That one?" said Henri's spouse. "He is of Montmartre! To him nothing is sacred. He has the mind of an ape."

"And is the story suited to the mind of an ape?"

"In effect, no. It is grotesque, not more. I think also that it is unfinished, but the little black lobster, I feel she has told what she knows."

Bluna's story began when she first took service with the professor at his lodgings. He had advertised for two Negro servants, preferably West Indians. Bluna and her fiancé, at that time unacquainted with one another, had come to Liverpool to find employment in England, and, in addition to some thirty other unemployed West Indians, had answered the advertisement. They had all been interviewed on the same day at a London lodging house of a type where payment in advance was the rule and no questions were asked.

Bluna had been chosen from among the women applicants because she had said that she could neither read nor write.

"All the same, madame, she tells me that this was a little fib to get the job, because she is intelligent, that one, and she knows the professor is no good, and may not want anybody who can become too much interested in his affairs. She likes not bad men, but she is in a bad way for money and must get some employment very quick."

The Negro man was chosen because he had served a prison sentence . . . justly, according to Bluna. He had been convicted in England, almost upon arrival, for theft. According to Bluna he was not an habitual criminal but he was desperate and had picked a couple of pockets.

The two newly appointed servants had then been given third-class tickets while the professor went first-class, and he took them by taxi from Wallchester station to his lodgings. His landlady had been much averse to taking them in but had been overridden by the professor who seemed, thought Bluna, to have some hold over her apart from his payment of rent.

"Soon after she arrived she began to find out that the professor was a bad man, but different from what she has believed, madame. He gives parties of a bizarre character at which she is to wait upon the guests naked."

"Fotis," murmured Mrs. Bradley, thinking again of the book of the Golden Ass.

"I do not know." Celestine dismissed the handmaid of Pamphiles from the matter in hand. "No violence of any kind, she says, was ever offered her, and the parties were of a great seriousness. Large books were consulted and there was much discussion. The guests were all young men except one, and that was the murdered Mr. Aumbry. Then he came no more, and in his place two young men, the Mr. Catfield and Mr. Waite. But Mr. Waite has authority over Mr. Catfield. He is the senior partner in the friendship and dominates Mr. Catfield, but is gay, always, and very amusing."

But one day, it appeared, the party was not held at Professor Havers' lodgings, and Bluna was not asked to attend it. The fiancé, however, was told to go, and upon his return he had described to Bluna what had happened.

"Yes," said Mrs. Bradley, interrupting. "We will get that later from Mr. Majestic himself. It will be more satisfactory."

"As madame pleases. That, then, is the end of the little history until came two young men who are staying here."

"Not quite the end. What about the doll that was supposed to represent Mr. Aumbry but which really represented the professor?"

"No doll was mentioned, madame."

"Interesting. Well, what did Bluna say about the visit of the two under-graduates?"

"She did not know Mr. Harrison but thought she might have seen Mr. Piper."

"And why did she think they had come if she did not mention the doll?"

"She thought they had a practical joke to play on Professor Havers."

"So they had, in a sense, I suppose. Thank you very much, Celestine. You have managed well."

"Madame is served," said her maid ironically. Mrs. Bradley cackled and signaled to the silent Henri to pour out more wine.

(3)

Harrison's confessions had been as useful as those of Bluna. Illuminating, the Chief Constable called them, but Mrs. Bradley, who needed the confessions only to confirm her own views, preferred the more prosaic adjective.

Harrison had begun with the reading party of three . . . Waite, Piper and himself . . . at Piper's home.

"Of course, I can see now that Peter and I were stooges," he declared, "but at the time it seemed rather jolly. Polly was older than we were . . . about ten years older, you know . . . and had knocked around and done pretty well in the war, and I suppose we were rather pleased to get him down to Peter's place. It all went merrily . . . I mean, we didn't do much reading but we talked a lot and Peter made a jolly good host . . . his father was in Scotland and the house was all our own . . . and then came this business of old Havers and the doll.

"We were lounging about one morning when Polly spotted the advertisement, and before I knew where I was we had pushed off to Wallchester and had got stuck with the job of re-stealing the diptych. The rest I expect you know."

"There are one or two points, my dear David, on which I should like some clear evidence. It was understood, I gather, that you would return to Mr. Piper's home for the night and then go straight to Merlin's Furlong?"

"I suppose that was the idea. It was what I thought we should do."

"Quite so. Instead of that, what did actually happen?"

"Eh? Oh, well, we didn't get there quite as soon as that. If you remember, we spent the first night at Waite's aunt's place . . ."

"Whose idea was that?"

"Well, Polly suddenly remembered her, you know, and thought we might as well drop in. Of course, we never dreamed of staying the night."

"*You* did not dream of it, you mean. What about the following night?"

"That was when we'd lost the way and landed up at Merlin's Fort. I told you we had to spend the time camping out. I bagged the car and the other two slept in the heather."

"And from Merlin's Fort, if one knows the shortcut over the hill, it is only four miles to Merlin's Castle where Professor Havers was murdered. And his death took place during the night that you three were camping out."

"Oh, but look here . . . !"

"I am only stating facts, am I not?"

"Well, yes, but . . . hang it! Why *should* Polly want to kill Havers?"

"That I have still to find out . . . or, rather, I know why he wanted to, but I have to get my findings confirmed. Have you grasped why Professor Havers was so anxious to get you three to Merlin's Furlong, by the way?"

"You mean it wasn't that he wanted the diptych back?"

"If I remember the previous evidence, Professor Havers' one aim and object was to accomplish the death of Mr. Aumbry. This he vowed and declared in front of you."

"Oh, Lord! And that's what you think he did?"

"I have little doubt of it."

"And intended to stick us with the murder?"

"It begins to look like that, does it not?"

"The old . . . I'm sorry, but I was about to remark . . ."

"Quite. Mr. Waite, however, outwitted him, I think."

"Good for Polly! You mean he intentionally kept us on the road until it was certain we could not have been accused of murdering Aumbry?"

"That, among other things. But wonder on, till truth make all things plain."

"This man is Pyramus," added Harrison idiotically. "I say, this throws a new light on old Polly, doesn't it?"

"A new light is not necessarily a better light," said Mrs. Bradley in the Victorian idiom.

(4)

Bluna's fiancé sighed.

"I am a marked man," he stated lugubriously.

"Quite so," Mrs. Bradley agreed with her usual incongruous cheerfulness. "Therefore, if you would help the police, you see . . ."

"I see." His earnest brown eyes searched her black ones. "And you will be my friend?"

"To some extent, yes."

"There are no conditions to friendship."

"Oh, yes, there are. I must be able to trust you as well as love you. That is the difference between two fundamental emotions."

"I see. What do you want me to tell you?"

"All about young Mr. Catfield."

"He was killed. I expect you know."

"Yes. What was the order of events?"

"I don't know."

"Wasn't it voodoo ritual?"

"Voodoo? No. It was quiet and orderly."

"No cockerel with its head bitten off?"

"Nothing like that. Just white man magic, I think."

"Tell me all about it."

"All ritual, like that other Socrates. You know? His throat was cut, then . . . a sponge."

"So they tried that, did they? What did they do with the body?"

"They took it to the common. An open cut-throat razor was beside it. It had his fingerprints. He could not be buried in a churchyard. He was buried in a grove of trees at his own home, but those of us who knew . . ."

"Who were those who were willing to risk taking the body from its grave and transferring it to Merlin's Fort?"

"The friends of the ghost of the departed."

"Among whom you number yourself?"

"Indeed, yes."

"And Bluna?"

"She go because I go. Some women are necessary."

"What for?"

Mr. Majestic waved his arms dramatically.

"They take the place of the witches and then the black man like them better than the witches, and so the witches have no power."

"Blah!" said Mrs. Bradley rudely. "Now, tell me: if Professor Havers had not been dead, would any of you have dared to remove Mr. Catfield's body?"

"Mr. Waite was one of the friends of the ghost, I think, but I do not know what to say to you in reply."

"And after the body had been removed from Titmouse, I saw you dancing and singing and waving torches around the new grave on Merlin's Fort."

"That, yes." He seemed relieved. "We celebrate the death of Professor Havers. We were glad to have him demised."

"Have him . . . ?"

"We were all glad," said Majestic, simply, "to have him dead. We thought Mr. Catfield had killed him and had wafted him there . . . there, to his own place."

"Did you really? You know, Mr. Majestic, I'm not sure that I believe a word you're saying. Tell me truthfully why Mr. Catfield's body was moved, and when."

"We moved it when we knew the professor was dead."

"Yes, but why?"

"Mr. Waite told us to move it."

"I repeat, Mr. Majestic, why? What did you think was the reason? Or did you know what Mr. Waite had in mind?"

"We could guess. Mr. Catfield had a good friend."

"Ah, yes. By whose orders was the monkey put into a room at Merlin's Castle?"

"Professor Havers wished it."

"Before he died, or after?"

Majestic looked terrified and said:

"The dolls' heads were also there because Professor Havers wished it, but I do not know what were his plans to do with them. The monkey, I think, was Mr. Piper."

"I see. All right, Mr. Majestic. Would you call yourself a sophisticated man?"

"Oh, yes. I am educated in U.S.A."

"Then tell me *exactly* what happened when Mr. Catfield was killed, and *where* it happened."

But Majestic had had enough. He turned and made for the door.

"And I do not accuse Mr. Waite," he stated, "of killing Professor Havers. I say Mr. Waite was a good and sincere friend to Mr. Catfield, and that is all, and he *wished* us to dance round the grave on Merlin's Fort. He said Mr. Catfield would have wished it. I think he was right. Mr. Catfield was avenged on Professor Havers. It was well that we should give him the ceremony of the torches."

(5)

"No," said Piper very deliberately, "I *don't* think Polly could have sneaked off that night we slept at Merlin's Fort in the heather, and then sneaked back again without waking me up. And I didn't wake up. And I'm a very light sleeper."

"Would you feel any surprise if you knew for certain that Mr. Waite had committed murder?"

"Not if he had committed it on a mad dog, but old Havers wasn't mad, and Polly didn't kill him."

"Do you believe in private vengeance?"

"I've never thought much about it."

"Did you know of the friendship between Mr. Waite and young Mr. Catfield?"

"Yes. Remember *Attendez et Voyez?*—Waite and C. No?"

"Were you friendly with Mr. Waite at the same time?"

"Moderately. I went to one of Havers' parties with him, as I think you've already been told."

"Only one?"

"Yes. I was bored. It wasn't my idea of fun."

"I see from reports of the inquest that there was no suggestion of foul play when Mr. Catfield's body was examined. Why did Mr. Waite suspect that his friend had been murdered?"

"You'd better ask him. I've no evidence at all that he did. And I may as well tell you, here and now, that I'm going to stick to my story that Polly never left Merlin's Fort that night."

"You tacitly admit that he may have done, then?"

"I don't admit anything. I'm simply going to say, if I'm asked, that we were so damned uncomfortable that night that we lay awake and talked. You won't get at Polly through me. If all I think about that old goat Havers is true, the world is well quit of him, whoever put him out."

"When the question of getting back the diptych first arose, weren't you surprised that Mr. Waite agreed to essay the task for Professor Havers?"

"No. Polly would do most things for a rag."

"Did you know he had written the advertisement himself?"

"No, of course not. I don't believe it, either. Old Havers would have been bound to smell a rat."

"I think he did, but I also think he saw the way to lead you three into a trap. No doubt he knew that Mr. Waite was a friend of yours."

"Yes, I can see that, of course." Piper's tone had altered. His nervous ill-temper had vanished. He sounded alert and interested. "You mean Havers went to Merlin's Furlong as soon as we'd left him that morning, killed old Aumbry and went to earth at Merlin's Castle. He expected us to charge into Merlin's Furlong much sooner than we actually did, so that it could be thought we'd been surprised by old Aumbry and had knocked him on the head in a fit of panic. Havers himself would have given evidence that we had intended to go to Aumbry's house, and, of course, our fingerprints would have confirmed him in what he said. Quite a pretty little idea, take it all round, but how do we know it's true?"

"We don't. It's a working hypothesis."

"Well, it certainly works. It would explain a good deal."

"There is only one major point which it would *not* explain," said Mrs. Bradley. "It would not tell us why you three saw Mr. Godfrey Aumbry coming away from Merlin's Castle that day."

"Godfrey Aumbry? But . . ."

"That manservant was Godfrey Aumbry, Mr. Piper."

"But why on earth did he let us think he was old Havers' man?"

"That is what I still have to find out. He is not the type to mislead people simply for the fun of it."

"Then he must have murdered Havers!"

"That is another working hypothesis, of course."

"But you still think it was Polly? Of course, old Polly had a marvelous war record, you know, and I think he found civilian life rather tame. That's why at first he teamed up with Havers' mob. But when he found out what they were up to—scientific experiments in witchcraft, old Havers called it, and, of course, it stank to high heaven—Polly oiled out. Besides, young Catfield's suicide opened his eyes pretty wide."

"Catfield's *suicide,* Mr. Piper?"

"There was an inquest, you know," said Piper gloomily. "I knew Polly never thought Catfield cut his own throat, but old Havers was pretty fly, and the verdict was suicide all right."

CHAPTER SIXTEEN

Merlin's Answer

"Fie upon him; he will discredit our mystery."

SHAKESPEARE—*Measure for Measure*

"It has often been laid down," said the Chief Constable, "that it is not only necessary to assemble all the available evidence; it is essential that it should then be read in the right order. Mrs. Bradley thinks (and I agree with her) that in the puzzling cases we have been investigating, the available evidence has at last been arranged logically, and, if we are right, then the cases are no longer puzzling but fall into the simple, and, in England, rather unusual, category of murders for revenge."

"Fairy-tale stuff!" said Frederick Aumbry, from the depths of an armchair. "It wouldn't be worth it. Only reason *I'd* ever commit murder would be for money, and even then I'd have to be pretty sure I could get away with plenty of it!"

"There speaks the man of rational mind," said Mrs. Bradley. "The trouble about these three crimes is that they were not rational except to the diseased brains by which they were prompted."

The conference was being held at Merlin's Furlong, now the property of Richmond Aumbry. He and his cousins and brother, the three undergraduates, Mrs. Bradley, the Chief Constable, Inspector Ekkers (whose patient and conscientious work had helped to establish Mrs. Bradley's theories as facts) were all present. Godfrey Aumbry, seated a little apart at a small table, had pens and paper before him . . . four beautifully cut quills and some admirable parchment . . . and had announced his intention of taking notes.

"The legal mind at work," said Lewis, who, pad on knee, was indulging a cherished hobby of making rapid caricatures of everybody in the room.

"I shall be interested to hear a *logical* argument stated by a psychiatrist," said Godfrey, his polite tones glossing over the venom of the words.

"My argument," Mrs. Bradley blandly observed, "is helped only partly by psychiatry. It will be best, I think, if I tell you all what I consider to be the unarguable facts and then what I deduce from them now that I have them in order. And yet . . ." She paused and gazed sternly at Waite, who had picked up the diptych and was gloating over its highly immoral interior, "I hesitate to appear tedious. Perhaps it would be preferable to all of you if I announced and analyzed those facts which, throughout the enquiry, have seemed at various times either inexplicable or capable of bearing two or more interpretations."

"Such as the extraordinary action of the late Mr. Aumbry in suddenly making a new will and appointing Mr. Richmond Aumbry instead of Mr. Godfrey Aumbry to be his heir?" suggested the Chief Constable.

"That was the second of those mystifying facts. The first was that Mr. Godfrey Aumbry was knocked on the head and his papers removed. I think there was a distinct connection between those two events, and I am going to suggest that one person among those present made that connection and made it correctly. That person, of course, was Mr. Godfrey Aumbry himself."

Godfrey nodded, and dipped a pristine quill in the ink.

"I didn't understand at first," he said, "but I understood all right when uncle made Richmond his heir."

"Quite so. The third apparently inexplicable fact is that Mr. Waite sent an obscurely worded advertisement to the newspapers under a ridiculous pseudonym, answered it himself as though he believed the late Professor Havers had inspired it, and took with him two innocent accomplices."

"Here, I say, though!" protested Piper.

"Shut up, Peter dear," said Waite. "Of course you were innocent, and, personally, I wouldn't even call you and David accomplices." He looked challengingly at Mrs. Bradley. She accepted the correction.

"Dupes, then," she said, grinning at the deeply offended Piper. Piper, who had brought his kitten to the meeting, cuddled it in injured silence. "The point is that, of the three, only Mr. Waite knew what was in the wind."

"But if this is all true," said Harrison, opening his eyes and then sighing and closing them again preparatory to continuing his twilight life of slumber, "why did old Havers fall for it?"

"He was fencing all the time, David," said Piper. "I can see that now. He must have realized that I'd once been to one of his damn silly parties. He was engaged in such nauseous stuff that he had to be careful, and anybody who'd ever had anything to do with him must have been a marked man thenceforward. In other words, I was the monkey."

"And, of course, he did want to get rid of that doll I'd sent him," said Waite. "He knew what it meant all right. It wasn't that he wanted *this* back." He closed the diptych and laid it on the carpet at his feet. "It belonged to Cat, you see. That's why he'd given it away. He was a superstitious old unprintable, you know. He really believed in most of that messy tripe he practiced. Anyway, if I'd known where it was I'd have sneaked it back long ago, but I'd burgled Havers' lodgings twice and Merlin's Castle three times (without any luck) before the three of us went there, so I guessed we shouldn't find it."

"What!" exclaimed Harrison. "Do you mean to say you knew that neighborhood all the time, and yet you led us that dance all over the place those two days?"

"Yes." Waite waved a thick, competent hand. "Mrs. Bradley will tell you, I'm sure. I'd rather she did, although how she found out I don't know."

"My conclusions there depended upon the fact that you could not have committed the first murder, that of Mr. Aumbry, and yet you went to his house. I studied the architecture of Merlin's Furlong very closely, and it seemed to me that, even though you had had no hand in Mr. Aumbry's death, you assumed that it had taken place. Merlin's Castle, with its absurd porch and broken window, was as easy to escape from as to break into, but Merlin's Furlong, with its twin towers and narrow staircases, its collegiate rooms and quadrangle, and its lane unsuitable for motors, was a different matter entirely. The owner, when you arrived, was either absent or dead, and since it seemed unlikely that you knew of the one (there was nothing at all except your knowledge of Professor Havers to connect you with the Aumbry family, and at no time did your companions, Mr. Piper and Mr. Harrison, indicate in their evidence either to me or to the police, that the professor had said that Mr. Aumbry's house would be empty) I assumed, as a working hypothesis, that you knew, or, at any rate, believed, that Mr. Aumbry was dead."

"Yes, I guessed old Havers had killed him and thought we should be accused because we should have been in the house at near enough the right time."

"Exactly. To circumvent Professor Havers, therefore, you dallied one night at your aunt's house and then, as Mr. Harrison complains, led your companions in 'a dark, uneven way' all over Moundshire, ending by forcing them to spend the second night at Merlin's Fort, Mr. Harrison in the car and the other two of you on the heather. I was suspicious about all this because, by what we learned from the evidence of Mr. Piper and Mr. Harrison, Mr. Piper was the best driver of the three, and yet, at all times, when the car lost its way, it appeared that you were driving it and that you refused advice about your route from the others."

"Quite right."

"So Professor Havers killed Mr. Aumbry," said Piper. "What was the reason if it wasn't to get back the diptych?"

"Revenge, you said," remarked Richmond Aumbry. "But what interests me, naturally, is why you didn't think *I* murdered Uncle Aumbry. *I'm* the person who had everything to gain by his death."

"I think you came to the conclusion that the altered will was no sudden whim, no cruel impulse, on the part of your uncle. You came to a realization that your uncle intended the new will to stand. It made sense of an otherwise senseless incident . . ."

"Old Godfrey being bonked over the conk and his papers pinched. I know," put in Frederick. "There was only one explanation of that. I can see it clearly. Uncle Aumbry himself must have clocked him."

"Yes. For some time Mr. Aumbry had been suspicious of the relationship between his nephew Godfrey and Professor Havers. But, apart from that melodramatic attack on Godfrey, he could not think of any way of getting evidence that they were plotting against him."

"Plotting? In what way?" demanded Godfrey, his quill spluttering angrily on the parchment. "You have to substantiate these statements. I am a lawyer, you know."

"Exactly. But that has nothing to do with the fact that you persuaded your uncle that there was a lucrative living to be earned by blackmail."

"Blackmail!"

"You discovered that Professor Havers and his circle had been concerned in the various sins and malpractices which led to the death of young Mr. Catfield, and it is of no use for you to deny the connection with Professor Havers, for you have been identified as the supposed manservant who was leaving Merlin's Castle when these three misguided young men first came to it."

"We all recognize him now, too," said Piper.

"They fabricated that story of the manservant to clear themselves," said Godfrey coldly. He stabbed his second quill violently upon his blotting paper and split the nib past remedy.

"No, the story was substantiated partly by the medical evidence which showed that death had taken place some time before these young men arrived, and partly through the untiring efforts of Inspector Ekkers and his men to trace that manservant. You chose a poor disguise, Mr. Aumbry. You see, a respectable manservant in morning clothes and a bowler, whatever his manner and his mode of speech (both of which you seem to have managed admirably) does not really *look* so very different from a respectable solicitor."

"I see," said Godfrey, sourly. "So I'm supposed to have murdered Havers and walked straight out into the arms of those three young idiots, am I?"

"One thing which made me extremely suspicious of Mr. Waite when I discovered that he had led the party such a dance over Moundshire," continued Mrs. Bradley, "was this business of sleeping in the heather. There was nothing, so far as I could see, to prevent Mr. Waite, who (we are now aware) knew the countryside intimately, from leaving Mr. Piper asleep and creeping away to the footpath which leads four miles over the hill to Merlin's Castle. He had plenty of time to walk the distance there and back, and kill Professor Havers, and again be in the heather by the time Mr. Piper woke up. But that wasn't what happened, was it? Would you like me to go on?"

Godfrey Aumbry, who had taken more notes, suddenly dropped his quill on the floor and bent to pick it up. It was the third he had used. Mrs. Bradley signaled violently to Piper, who was sitting nearest to Godfrey, and Piper, for years accustomed to interpreting the essential S.O.S. codes of his less intelligent friends, picked up the unused quill and began to tease the kitten with the feathered end of it.

"*Thank* you!" said Godfrey, making a furious snatch; but Piper eluded him easily and passed the quill to the Chief Constable. The latter weighed it in his hand, looked hard at Godfrey, and then said quietly:

"Do you mind if I take the feathered top off this pen, Mr. Aumbry?"

"So he dished himself by carrying a lethal dose about with him," said Harrison. "But you never suspected anyone else, I suppose, and that's why you tumbled to the pens and watched him so carefully all the time."

"Dear me! You see a great deal through those closed eyelids, Mr. Harrison!"

"One thing I *did* see," said Harrison, "that I don't propose to tell anybody."

"I will tell you what you saw. You saw Mr. Waite returning to the heather in the early morning. But he hadn't come from Merlin's Castle, you know. He'd come from visiting the top of Merlin's Fort. He had already made up his mind to give Mr. Catfield what he considered an honorable burial up there. He had also decided upon his helpers, whom he knew he could threaten into obeying him. But of this I shall say nothing to anybody but you. Mr. Catfield had never been buried in consecrated ground and therefore the crime of body-snatching need not come into the affair. Whatever Mr. Waite's faults, he loved his friend, and wished, in his perverted way, to do him honor. Possibly you remember his gesture of defiance to old Mr. Catfield in tossing a dead cat on to the rifled grave? It was probably old Mr. Catfield's evidence at the inquest which prevented the jury from adding the merciful rider of "while the balance of his mind was disturbed" to their verdict of suicide.

"Possibly also you remember that Mr. Waite would not meet old Mr. Catfield that day? He had two reasons for that. The second one was that he knew the old gentleman would recognize him and perhaps put two and two together in the matter of the removal of the body."

"But how did you manage to tie Polly up with all this?"

"I was certain of it when I recognized him as the driver of one of the coaches which had brought the fire-dancers to the top of Merlin's Fort. I had earlier formed the theory that Mr. Waite had two ulterior motives in spending that Thursday night with you and Mr. Piper at the Fort, and the discovery of the displaced and replaced turf, when you, George and I visited the Fort later on, seemed to fit this theory."

"Golly! Are you clairvoyant?" muttered Harrison.

"Oh, no. I have no supernatural gifts, but it is my business to find out what goes on in people's minds, and I found Mr. Waite an interesting study."

"And old Polly really blackmailed all those followers of Havers into going up there and dancing round the grave?"

"He had them in the hollow of his hand. He knew all about them, you see. The dancing was, to him, I think, a combination of ritual for his dead friend and his idea of a rag. I deduce that he was influenced by these conflicting thoughts as he himself did not join the dancers nor suffer blistered feet as they did."

"Well, it's been all of a queer do," said Harrison. "How did you *know* it was Godfrey Aumbry who had killed Havers?"

"I could not be absolutely certain until the episode of the poison-filled feather, child."

"Good Lord! You've got a neck!"

"Like Mr. Churchill's chicken, yes. But *you* haven't, and so I should advise you to steer clear of Mr. Waite from now onwards. He is born to trouble as the sparks fly upwards, and it's no thanks to him that you and Mr. Piper are not in prison. And there's another thing you must remember. Mr. Waite knew perfectly well that he'd taken you to Merlin's Castle instead of to Merlin's Furlong that first time."

"Yes, I know he did. But why did he do it? He said it was to look for the diptych."

"He wanted to find out whether Professor Havers was in the house . . . and, of course, he went into the coach house and found the body while you were exploring upstairs."

"Oh . . . I see. Well, how *does* Godfrey Aumbry come into it?"

"Godfrey felt certain . . . remember he knew them both very well indeed . . . that Professor Havers had killed Mr. Aumbry to get rid of a blackmailer, and Godfrey was beside himself with fury. Although he knew that his uncle had found out his connection with the professor, he thought that, with time on his side, he might be able to get back into favor. He killed Havers out of revenge, and when he ran into the three of you (when you thought he was the manservant) he had come out of the Castle after clearing up any traces he might have left behind him. Murderers will do it. They never will leave well alone."

"And it was Frederick Aumbry who came to Merlin's Furlong that night while Peter had gone for the police?"

"Exactly. He proposed to break in and steal, but Frederick has an excellent sense of *sauve qui peut* and did not wait upon his going once he realized that the house was occupied."

"What's going to happen to Polly now?"

"Nothing. He will one day hoist himself with his own petard. There is not much doubt about that. I do not think Mr. Waite is of the type that lives and learns."

"He's never settled down since the war. He was an ace pilot, you know."

"I can believe it readily. Mr. Piper said the same thing."

"And it's all due to you that all three of us aren't in jug—if nothing worse!"

"Yes, and none of you deserves my good offices," said Mrs. Bradley with an asperity she seldom showed to the young. "And next time you can all go and be hanged!"

Harrison fell on his knees and paid her homage.

> "Cynthia's shining orb was made
> Heaven to clear when day did close;
> Bless us, then, with wished sight,
> Goddess excellently bright."

"Never again," said Mrs. Bradley firmly.

THE END

About the Rue Morgue Press

"Rue Morgue Press is the old-mystery lover's best friend,
reprinting high quality books from the 1930s and '40s."
—*Ellery Queen's Mystery Magazine*

Since 1997, the Rue Morgue Press has reprinted scores of traditional mysteries, the kind of books that were the hallmark of the Golden Age of detective fiction. Authors reprinted or to be reprinted by the Rue Morgue include Catherine Aird, Delano Ames, H. C. Bailey, Morris Bishop, Nicholas Blake, Dorothy Bowers, Pamela Branch, Joanna Cannan, John Dickson Carr, Glyn Carr, Torrey Chanslor, Clyde B. Clason, Joan Coggin, Manning Coles, Lucy Cores, Frances Crane, Norbert Davis, Elizabeth Dean, Carter Dickson, Eilis Dillon, Michael Gilbert, Constance & Gwenyth Little, Marlys Millhiser, Gladys Mitchell, James Norman, Stuart Palmer, Craig Rice, Kelley Roos, Charlotte Murray Russell, Maureen Sarsfield, Margaret Scherf, Juanita Sheridan and Colin Watson..

To suggest titles or to receive a catalog of Rue Morgue Press books write 87 Lone Tree Lane, Lyons, CO 80540, telephone 800-699-6214, or check out our website, www.ruemorguepress.com, which lists complete descriptions of all of our titles, along with lengthy biographies of our writers.